K-GIRLS

K-Girls

FIRST IN THE
KYLEMORE ABBEY SCHOOL
SERIES

Lydia Little

LITTLE RED GATE

In memory of Ruth Stoker
and Dame Mary O'Toole,
K-Girls infinite.

Dedicated to every true K-Girl,
Here's to finding your own K-essence within.
PAX.

I'm nobody!   Who are you?
Are you nobody, too?
Then there's a pair of us – don't tell!
They'd banish us, you know.
Emily Dickinson

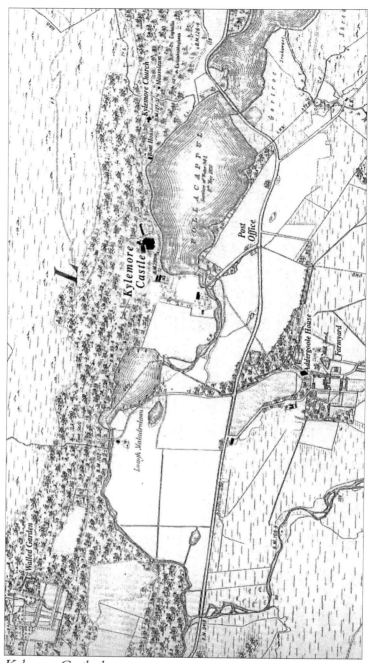

Kylemore Castle demesne.

Prologue

December 1923

John-Joe climbed out of the freshly dug grave. He had turned his hand to many a trade while working at Kylemore Castle, but this was something he never thought he would be called to do. Taking off his cap and wiping the sweat from his brow, his heart saddened as he looked down into the gaping pit.

'You finished there, Young Joe?' The slow, deep voice of Reilly, the head gardener, broke John-Joe's thoughts.

'Yes, Sir, just,' John-Joe replied as he took up his jacket from where he had tossed it earlier. He didn't usually like being called Young Joe, but Reilly had as good as raised him on the estate and John-Joe afforded Reilly the respect of not letting him know his own feelings on the matter. John-Joe's eyes glanced back towards the grave and spied some disturbed worms as they wriggled back into the damp mound of soil that would soon cover an innocent's life. He glanced away quickly.

'Any news on her, Sir?' John-Joe quietly asked.

'No, she's a tough little fighter, but it won't be long now. There's no winning this one. Her spirit's near lost. Father Donovan has given her the last rites. May God have mercy on her young soul.' Reilly blessed himself.

''Tis an awful shame, Sir, an awful shame.' John-Joe shook his head and blessed himself twice.

'Indeed, son, that it is, and not something Mother Superior will be happy about. All for good reason; there is the nuns to think about, and all them young ladies. Hopefully they've

1

been sent home in good time. It's not a good omen for the new school that is for sure.'

John-Joe thought back on the rushed travel arrangements and chaos that had followed Mother Superior's decision to evacuate the girls. 'It's just a shame it has to be like this, so quick like. No kin to send her on her way, and with it being so close to Christmas.'

'You're right there, Joe, you are right in that.'

Reilly started for the cemetery gate. John-Joe picked up his step in line with him and, feeling the winter air chill his damp shirt, he pulled on his jacket.

'Her parents requested that she'd be buried here, they can't make the funeral,' Reilly added.

Can't or won't? John-Joe thought, but didn't say.

'Paddy says we should use lime, Sir?' John-Joe didn't look Reilly in the eye when he asked it, and then added, 'On the grave, like.'

Reilly straightened his shoulders and dispelled the image John Joe had planted in his head. He increased his stride and thought of the more pleasant image of the gardens.

'Roses, Joe,' Reilly declared. 'The coming spring will have the best the gardens have seen yet. The Italian garden will be a feast of colour for the eye. Them trenches have worked well. Speaking of which, there is a problem with one of the mountain water pipes, it needs your fixing.' Reilly stepped up onto the donkey-drawn cart. 'Wants fixing this side of noon Joe,' he added impatiently.

John-Joe climbed up onto the cart next to Reilly and with a quick jerk of the reins Reilly had them on their way, away from the cemetery, back towards the castle and landscaped gardens beyond.

The slow rhythm of the donkey's step matched that of John-Joe's saddened heart. His mind wandered back to the little grave: a dark place to end your days, far from home and family. The only child to be buried in the nuns' new cemetery. And the saddest part for John-Joe was thinking of the girl in isolation in one of the old castle bedrooms, still alive, just, with her little heart slowly beating its way towards stopping. He decided he would call in on her. Take his chances. If he was going to be the last to see her dead, he would at least pay his respects while she was still alive. And by God's will he would make sure that the last face she saw would be a friendly one.

CHAPTER I

Boarding School

1983

'No way! You can't be serious?' Alice Stone stood gaping at her parents, stunned by the news that she was going to boarding school.

It was February, and the local secondary schools in the seaside town of Kinsale had been advertising their open days. Alice was in her final months in primary school and the time was fast approaching when she needed to book a place in a secondary school. All the rest of her class had already found places in the local schools, but Alice had different ideas.

Alice was bored, she sought adventure. And she felt she wasn't going to get it in the two local schools that were on offer, the Convent and the Tech. She had had this fantasy of boarding school after reading novels about girls who got to make a fresh start away from their parents, where there were lots of sports and midnight feasts, troublesome twins and after-school adventures. Of course, she didn't tell her parents that was why she wanted to go away. She pushed the idea of the extra sports and subjects that the local schools didn't do.

'Well, when you first put the idea of boarding school to us it was a bit of a surprise, to be honest,' Alice's mother said. 'But you just wouldn't stop going on about it.'

'Normally it's parents who threaten boarding school to their children,' Alice's dad joked. 'Not the other way around.'

Alice's mother smiled. 'Your father and I have been talking and, well, we're happy to go along with the idea if you're still keen.'

★★★

Later, Alice leaned over the big dining table where brochures on a variety of boarding schools were scattered. Some schools she eliminated straight away, simply from the picture of the school or how boring their prospectus was. Alice was looking through the pile trying to find one she had seen earlier, the one that she thought would give her the adventure she was looking for. The whole package. Somewhere different, where she could be away from her small-town life. There were some schools where you only boarded during the week and had to come home at weekends. Alice thought that idea sounded boring.

'Sure, where would the fun be in that?' Alice asked her buddy Pete as he stood looking absently at the brochures on the table. 'You'd be just there when you'd have to come home again.'

'Are all these boarding schools?' he asked innocently. 'I didn't think Ireland had so many.'

'Yeah, but as it turns out there are only a few that I can go to,' she explained as she shuffled through the pile.

'You mean there are only a few that would take you.' He gave Alice a friendly shove.

'Hah, very funny. You'll be the last to laugh when I am away and you are stuck in school with no one to hang out with.'

'It's not like you're my only friend, you know,' grumbled Pete. 'Anyway, who in their right mind wants to go to boarding school?'

Alice wasn't listening. Finding what she was looking for, she turned around, flashing a brochure in front of Pete's face. 'Here it is, this is it.' Alice held it up, jumping up and down excitedly.

5

'Would you stop bouncing, and show it to me a minute?' Pete grabbed the slim booklet from Alice and scanned through it.

'Kylemore Abbey School for Girls,' Pete read out aloud. 'Doesn't look up to much to me.' He made a face, and threw it back on the table.

Alice grabbed it back again.

'What do you mean? Look at the picture at the front. It's a castle. A CASTLE, Pete. And it has its own lake. I think it looks amazing. Like something out of a fairytale. AND they do gymnastics there, and dancing, and hockey, and volleyball. They even compete with other schools.'

Alice then added: 'I'm going to change my name, too.'

'You're what?'

'Yeah, you know how I have always hated my name?'

'Not that again.' Pete rolled his eyes.

'Well, I think this is the perfect time to do it. A new start.'

'And how are you going to go about doing that?' Pete sneered.

'You're just jealous'

'Am not,' he muttered.

Alice ignored him, scanning through the brochure.

'Oh and look at all the subjects that I can do. There's even Spanish, German and Latin, although I am not sure what I might think of the Latin, but Chemistry sounds like it could be fun.' Alice didn't bother to notice that Pete wasn't looking at the brochure anymore. Or that he wasn't smiling.

'Dad said he was going to contact the school to arrange an interview. Crikey, I have no idea what that might involve. I'm so nervous already, I wonder if he's called them?' She left the room in a flurry, calling out for her mother and abandoning the brochures and a very dispirited looking Pete.

CHAPTER 2

Connemara

And so it was arranged. Alice was to go to Connemara for an interview at Kylemore Abbey School for Girls.

The journey felt painfully long. But Alice did not want to let on. After all, if she was to start moaning and giving out now, what hope would she have of being able to go for the next six years?

Six years, Alice thought to herself. *I hope the other girls like me. I hope I like them. What if Mallory Towers was all nonsense? What if the school is awful, what if the teachers are rotten? What if . . .?*

'How many hours did you say it would take, Dad?' Alice put a perky note in her voice just to pretend how long it was actually taking didn't really bother her much. 'Oh we have a bit more to go, love. We've only just left Limerick. Why don't you close your eyes and have a sleep. I'll wake you when we're nearly there.'

Alice closed her eyes. At first she couldn't sleep, but soon the rhythm of the driving and the sound of the engine lulled her, and her eyes felt heavy. She became so comfortably tired that she fell asleep.

A sudden jolt woke her. Alice wiped the sleep from her eyes and looked out the car window. They were in the middle of nowhere, driving alone along a narrow, never-ending road that cut through a deep barren-looking valley. Her father weaved around the stretches of road polka-dotted with potholes. Alice's eyes followed the line of mountains that stretched as far as her eye could see. She found it hard to believe that there was a school out here.

At last they left the valley and took a slow turn across a man-made causeway that divided a lake in two. And then out of the nothingness there it was. A magnificent castle with high walls, turrets and towers sat on the edge of the lake beneath the shadow of the mountain; looking back at it was a crystal-clear reflection of itself in the lake. It looked so out of place and yet perfect. Alice was awestruck.

Alice's dad had slowed down as they passed over the causeway so that they could all take in the sight before them. Both parents smiled to each other as they listened to Alice's gasp.

For a child who always had something to say, they both hoped it was a good sign.

★★★

Alice couldn't take her eyes off the castle. The reality of boarding school hit her. She suddenly felt unworthy. Surely all the girls that go there would be way too posh for her, she would never fit in. Her stomach rolled with nausea. There she was, the last few weeks totally convinced that she wanted to go to boarding school, and now she found herself actually quite terrified of the idea.

They lost sight of the castle behind a thick wall of rhododendrons. Flickers of sunlight speckled through the hedge, dancing about like fairies and teasing her with what secret pleasures the place might have for her. And then hidden partly by the hedgerow were the welcome sign and entrance gate. They had finally arrived.

A cosy little cottage with white wooden fencing and pretty garden sat to the right of the entrance with a sign for Post Office and Telephone.

'How quaint,' Alice's mum commented.

They turned in and with the clank of cattle grids they

drove through the low-slung green gates. 'They wouldn't do much to keep a girl in now, would they?' Dad joked.

A good omen, Alice hoped.

Alice's father slowed as they got closer to the castle and parked at the base of the parapet. After they disentangled themselves from the car, Alice felt the cool breeze carrying wafts of crisp mountain air. Voices were caught on the wind and brought a new wave of excitement and anticipation to Alice's stomach. Her mother finished preening herself, then turned to Alice and, while they walked, she brushed Alice's shoulders and combed her hair into place. She pushed her mother's hand away impatiently; Alice's focus was on the impressive castle.

There were the tall towers, big windows and castellated walls. Alice felt a strange sort of yearning in her gut, drawing her forward. She could not have described it much more than a feeling that she was *home*. All the worry of being at boarding school and the fuss and bother that she had created in trying to get into one just seemed to wash away from her now. In fact she knew in that instant that she wanted to attend *this* school, and to do that she would have to pass the interview.

In that moment a new gnawing sensation hit her gut. Now she was really nervous. Now it mattered what they thought of her. Now it mattered that she made a good first impression.

They walked on slowly and Alice's eyes scanned the castle front. It seemed to grow taller as they approached. She found her eyes wandering up past the doorway to the tower above it, dotted with Gothic windows. A quick movement caught her eye in a window higher up. There was someone there looking down on them. Alice squinted to try and focus. Between the brightness of the day and the distance to the tower, she wasn't sure, but she thought she could just make out a girl watching them. A strange déjà vu sensation passed over her. She met and held the girl's gaze, and for a moment something passed between them. Alice smiled, but as soon as she did, the girl was gone.

CHAPTER 3

Dame Mary

Alice's father gripped the large round old handle of the front door and had to give it a twist and a shove to enter. Stepping in from the brightness of the day, Alice took a moment to adjust her eyes to the darkness of the hallway. It was cooler in here. A calming silence, mingled with the smell of wood and polish, enveloped them. Instinctively, Alice went quiet.

There was wood everywhere, lining the walls and floor, and even in the form a large carved statue. Alice looked briefly into the lifeless eyes of the man holding a book and crozier. Walking in further, Alice noticed a nun sitting at a desk at the other side hall.

'Gosh, she looks fairly sober.' Alice whispered to her mum. Alice's mum suppressed a laugh at Alice's word misuse and whispered quickly, 'I'm sure you mean sombre, dear'.

Her parents wandered over to the nun. Alice held back and waited. Some tourists mingled around the hall looking at religious pamphlets and peering into glass cases that lined the wall under a grand winding staircase. Alice was curious and wanted to go a bit closer to see for herself, but just then her mother called her over.

The nun was dressed in a full traditional habit with long black veil and white trim head band that hugged her round, pink cheeks. Alice thought she might have been pretty except for the blank staring eyes that watched Alice as she approached.

'Alice, this is Sister Valentine.'

Alice's mum gave her a look that Alice recognised well.

It was her come-now-Alice-be-polite-and-don't-let-me-down look. Alice stepped towards the nun, giving her one of her best staged smiles, and suddenly realised she had no idea how to greet a nun. *Do you shake hands or is there some special rule when it comes to meeting a holy person?* Alice stopped. She thought it best to rely on good manners.

'Hello, Sister Valentine, nice to meet you.' Alice extended her hand nervously towards the nun. The nun appeared to be armless, but then one shot out from behind her tunic and took Alice's own extended hand. The nun's hand felt limp and clammy. She smiled insincerely at Alice and nodded. Alice returned a forced smile, then glanced at her parents. They were pretending to smile too.

It seemed an age before someone said something. Then Sister Valentine spoke.

'Welcome, Alice.' Her voice was high-pitched and nasal. 'Dame Mary is expecting you. If you follow me I will let her know you have arrived.' With this she glided towards a white wooden door with a brass plate marked *Library* on it, and showed them into a large bright room.

'Please take a seat, and Dame Mary will be with you shortly.'

Dame Mary? Alice gave her parents a puzzled look. She might have asked, but the beauty of the room distracted her. It was as if they had stepped back in time to the days when the abbey was a castle.

Beautiful long windows overlooked the parapet at the front and the lake and mountain beyond. The Library was everything you might expect, except the most obvious. There were no books. The centrepiece of the room was a fine white-marble fireplace with carved figurines of angelic young women holding up the mantelpiece on each side. The furniture was all antique save for a couple of sets of red-leather three-piece suites. which stood out starkly against the rest of the contents.

Alice supposed that this was where they were to sit and headed towards them with her parents. A large portrait of a beautiful lady in a wonderful pink gown glanced down on her as she passed beneath. It was the only hanging picture in the room. Alice felt as if the lady's eyes followed her as she walked by.

Alice was just getting comfortable in the couch when the door of the Library opened again, and in walked Sister Valentine accompanying another nun.

Alice felt an immediate attraction for the new arrival. She looked older than Sister Valentine, with a warm rosy-cheeked, big round face that nestled in the confines of her wimple and veil. She played music as she walked, a chain of keys jangling somewhere beneath her tunic, swinging like a pendulum in rhythm with her step across the room. The nun's eyes sparkled behind a pair of small round glasses, and Alice couldn't help but notice a missing tooth as the nun beamed a wide, genuinely warm smile at them. Sister Valentine introduced the nun as Dame Mary. Alice was surprised at being greeted first. She had assumed that the outstretched hand had been for either of her parents

'Oh!' said an embarrassed Alice. 'Pleased to meet you.' Taking the nun's hand, Alice found herself curtsying.

Now what on earth made me do that? The last time she had curtsied was at ballet class when she was six. Alice parents were staring at her. Dame Mary paused, smiled, and quickly moved on to formally greet Alice's stunned parents.

CHAPTER 4

Interview

'You had a good journey I take it?' Dame Mary asked as she sat in a single chair opposite them.

'Yes, thank you, it was long, but the Connemara landscape made it all worthwhile,' Alice's father replied. 'You have a beautiful place here, Sister Mary.'

'I noticed few girls around, are there many girls boarding here, *Dame* Mary? Alice's mum glanced at her husband.

'We are an intimate school. In all we currently have one hundred and seventy students, with around one hundred of those being boarders. The grounds are quiet now as the girls are at study.'

Alice remembered the girl she saw in the tower. 'Oh, do the girls get to study in the towers?' she asked excitedly.

Dame Mary turned to face Alice. 'No my dear, the towers are *strictly* out of bounds to the girls.' Turning to Alice's parents, she added, 'No, junior girls study in the main study hall, and the seniors in their own classrooms. There are two supervised study periods per day. There is no study on a Friday.' She said this while looking at Alice with a big smile. 'That is when we have assembly and free time. The girls use the time to get some fresh air or socialise in the common areas.'

Alice wondered about the girl she had seen in the tower and, smiling to herself, guessed she was probably mitching study period. She liked the idea of that. Sitting upright and knees together, Alice was determined to make a good first impression.

Her mother kept looking at her strangely, trying to decide what changeling had taken the place of her tomboy daughter who usually wouldn't stop talking and constantly jigged on the spot.

It wasn't long before tea and cake arrived, delivered by Sister Valentine. Dame Mary poured and served Alice a slice of tea brack along with cup of tea in a delicate cup with saucer. Alice was stumped. She did not like brack unless it was spread with a thick smear of butter, and as for tea, well, she didn't like that much at all. But what she really dreaded was what she might do with it served in a cup and saucer. Not wanting to appear childish or rude, she accepted both and was quick enough not to reach for the milk jug but waited to be offered, giving a short tap-tap of her spoon after mixing. Then she sipped silently with her pinky finger extended enough to be noticed but not cocky. The bitter taste of tannin stuck to the top of her mouth. She had forgotten to add sugar and guessed it was too late to go adding some now. Alice bit a corner of the brack and tried in vain to suck enough saliva into her mouth to moisten its dry fruity taste. She froze as Dame Mary put a serious question to her.

'You are a long way from family and friends here, Alice, do you think you would miss them too much if you were to attend Kylemore?'

The little bit of moisture in her mouth had evaporated, so so she took a sip of tea to wet its contents, swallowed and took another moment to place her cup and saucer.

Summoning up all the etiquette she could muster, Alice answered, 'I am sure I would miss them all greatly, in the beginning, but am equally sure that I will make new friends here, so that between school and sports the time would pass quickly until I would be home again for the holidays.'

Dame Mary nodded approvingly. Alice inhaled with relief and, with a quick glance at her parents sitting proudly, she felt quite chuffed with her self.

Sister Valentine returned to the room again. 'Excuse me, Dame Mary. The girls are waiting in the hall.' She left as silently as she had arrived.

Dame Mary turned to Alice and her parents, and explained: 'Alice, I thought it would be a good idea for some of the Second Years to give you a tour of the grounds while I have a little chat with your parents.'

Alice looked to her mother who nodded, and excusing herself she made her way to the door.

Three girls stood in a line and waited for her to approach. They were all dressed the same, yet different. Each wore the same grey skirt, white knee socks, navy jumper with v-neck and a little blue and white chequered blouse collar peeping over the 'V'. Their differences were in their sizes and self-styled adaptation of the uniform.

One towered over the others with lengths of blond, curly hair down her back. Alice had never seen the like. It reminded her of her nursery book at home and the story of Goldilocks, only this one was a giant Goldilocks. Everything looked that just little bit short on her: her skirt not quite meeting her knees, her socks mid-calf and her jumper sleeves mid-wrist. *Looks like this Goldilocks had a massive growth spurt over night.* Alice subdued a smile at the thought.

The other two were dark haired. Alice thought one looked foreign, with her dark skin, black hair and her dark, almond-shaped eyes. The girl was extremely tidy in her appearance. Her long glossy hair was pulled back tightly in a very neat ponytail. She had her very white knee-socks pulled up to the knee and was wearing new-looking deck shoes. The short-haired girl looked rather boyish and unkempt with sloppy socks, an over-sized jumper and well-worn scuffed deck shoes.

The three grinned at Alice as she approached. They were

certainly not the posh, snobby type of girls she had been expecting to meet. Goldilocks spoke first.

'Hi, I'm Mary-Jane, this is Felicity,' she pointed to the short haired untidy looking girl. 'And this is Ting,' pointing to the foreign looking girl. All three nodded at Alice.

'Hi.' Alice hesitated, wondering if she should shake hands or something, but then felt awkward and pretended to tuck her hair behind her ears.

'You're looking to start in September?' Mary-Jane asked.

'Yes, but I suppose it's not guaranteed yet. My folks are in with Sister, I mean Dame, Mary right now still discussing it.'

'Oh I wouldn't worry about that,' said Felicity. 'Dame Mary is a sweetie and it would take a real eejit not to make it into Kylemore. Where're you from by the way?'

'Cork,' Alice replied, adding, 'What is a Dame?'

'Oh, sorry for your trouble. Being from Cork, that is. I'm from Killarney,' Felicity announced with pride, then added 'not sure about the Dame thing.' Some of the nuns go by Sister, and I think the older ones go by Dame, but Dame Mary is the only one we actually call Dame. We don't have much interaction with the old ones.'

Here Ting piped in. 'I think Dame is an old term from the nuns' time in Ypres, you know, in Belgium. They had to escape during World War One and came here to set up a new Abbey. The Dames were the educated nuns and paid a dowry, and Sisters were the poorer working lay nuns. Vatican Two changed all that. They don't differentiate between them now. Except with Dame Mary. I think it just kind of stuck. She goes by Sister Mary too but I think likes being called Dame by the students.'

Mary Jane and Felicity looked to their friend and rolled their eyes. 'Ting here is a bit of a know-it-all,' Mary-Jane said. 'But we'll forgive her for it.' Ting ignored her.

'I'm from Dublin, by the way,' added Mary-Jane. 'Ting is from Tokyo.' At this Ting bowed.

'Wow, that's cool,' remarked Alice.

'*Arigato,*' Ting said, thanking her in perfect Japanese and bowing again. Alice was charmed.

Mary-Jane was about to go on but Felicity interrupted. 'Sister Valentine said to give you a tour of the grounds, get some fresh air, stretch your legs after being stuck in the car all day. Will you go back today or are you over-nighting?'

'No, we're to go back today. I'm not looking forward to the return trip. Gosh, you really are in the boonies here, aren't you?'

'Know the feeling, but you get used to that. And believe me, the journey seems twice as long when going home for the holidays!'

'Are you all Second Years?' asked Alice, looking at the full height of Mary-Jane.

'Yes, even daddy-long-legs here,' teased Felicity. Ting sniggered. Mary-Jane stuck out her tongue at her.

They left the hall and Abbey behind them and soon were strolling along under a canopy of trees that continued to follow the path along the lake on one side and the mountain undergrowth on the other. The conversation generally covered things like what it was like to go to school at the Castle, what the teachers were like and fun things they did in their free time. Alice discovered that the Abbey didn't have enough space to accommodate all the girls.

'I suppose you could say it is a general rule that First Years and exam students sleep in the Abbey, with a choice of Abbey or Farm being given to other years,' Ting explained.

'The Farmers are escorted every evening to the Farm and are strongly supervised,' Ting added. 'They have to share bedrooms and the sinks. There are no showers there, just baths.'

Ting sniffed indignantly. 'We are Abbey-ers. We have our own cubicles, shower facilities and are closer to the class-rooms and study halls.'

'Yeah, we really like being closer to the study halls,' Mary-Jane said sarcastically.

'Nah, it's more like we prefer to be closer to the af-ter-hours fun and action,' Felicity said. Alice smiled, liking the sound of that.

The three girls competed with stories and accounts of what they had done in their short history at Kylemore, with midnight feasts, swimming in the rock pools and silly pranks on each other. Alice could hardly contain her excitement. Everything she was hearing was exactly what she was hoping for. Ting offered a titbit every now and then, usually to cor-rect or impart some facts on the school's history.

'The castle was built by the Henry family around the 1860s,' Ting stated. 'Mitchell Henry built it as a wedding present for his wife, Margaret. But she died from Nile Fever while on holiday in Egypt.'

'Oh, how awful!' Alice was captivated.

'Yeah,' piped in Mary-Jane, 'that's why he built the Gothic and the Mausoleum. In her memory.'

Alice didn't know what a mausoleum was but didn't let on and merely nodded. Ting went on to explain.

'There had originally been a fishing lodge here, where Mitchell and Margaret spent their honeymoon. Margaret loved the area and apparently asked Mitchell if they could buy a house somewhere close by. Well, he bought the lodge and *fifteen thousand* acres. It was soon enough after the Famine, and the land and people were in a bad way. The estate gave great employment to the area. The Henrys were well-liked as landlords apparently, but when Margaret died, Mitchell was heartbroken and gave up. He retuned to England, not wanting to have the memory of her here, I suppose. Eventually he sold Kylemore. I think some duke bought it then but didn't have it too long. He was a gambler and couldn't keep up with the costs of the place. He was forced to sell it. That's where the nuns come in. They had come to Ireland looking for a new place to base their convent. Kylemore was perfect for them, and they got it cheap enough, been here since.'

Alice was enchanted. It was more than she could have imagined.

'So that portrait in the Library of the woman in the pink dress, that's Mrs Henry?'

'Yeah, when she died, Mitchell Henry buried her in the Mausoleum. Planted ten trees for each of their children around it.'

'Ten kids? I thought it was eight,' Mary-Jane frowned.

'Eight, ten, what does it matter, she had lots!' Ting tutted impatiently.

'Worst part is that they say she never got to see the completion of the castle,' Felicity added.

'All that time building something for someone and they drop dead,' Mary-Jane laughed. 'What a waste of money.'

'Not quite, Mary-Jane,' Ting corrected again. Mary Jane crossed her arms defiantly.

'The castle was finished in time all right, and Margaret did get to spend a few years here. She didn't actually drop dead. Nile fever kills you slowly over days. There was no quick death for her.' Alice thought how horribly romantic and sad.

CHAPTER 5
The Gothic

The three girls led Alice along the meandering path until there was an opening ahead where, enclosed by a dense growth of bushes, there stood a little church with a tall, square tower. 'Oh, what *is* that?' Alice quickened her pace towards what seemed to her like a miniature cathedral. The three Second Years smiled at each other.

'That's the Gothic,' Felicity said. 'It's not used anymore, all shut up. But it's nice to come here for a walk during free time.'

'Wow.' Alice craned her neck up to the tall steeple and tower, squinting at the stone carved gargoyles that grimaced down at her.

'That's what Mitchell Henry built in memory of his wife after she died,' said Ting. 'I think the family used it for a while but the nuns don't. It's too far for them to come for their daily Mass and prayers, so they built a chapel in the Abbey instead. Can you believe they converted the old ballroom into a church?'

'It's lovely.' Alice made her way up to the small porch entrance and the double-arched doors, hoping to go in.

'Oh you won't be able to go in.' Ting came up behind Alice. 'The nuns have it chained. You'd have to face Martin if you were caught in there.'

'Who's Martin?'

'That would be Sister Martin,' Mary-Jane explained. 'You don't mess with her. She's like the grounds gamekeeper and vet, works with the horses and organises all the workers.'

'Martin is a nun?' Alice turned in surprise.

'Calamity-Jane in a Habit,' Ting stated.

'We see her every now and then with the shotgun,' Mary-Jane explained. 'Seriously scary, we stay well away from her.'

Alice made a mental note to look out for Sister Martin. She leant against the two doors to the Gothic. A thick chain was wrapped around the doors' looped handles. She was startled when the chain slipped enough to offer a gap into the church interior. A thick musty smell wafted out through the opening, and Alice took a sudden step back onto Ting's foot.

'Ow!' Ting exclaimed.

Alice muttered an embarrassed apology.

'No worries. Legs here does it all the time.' Ting nodded towards Mary-Jane.

'Hey,' Mary-Jane scowled. Ting quickly lost her smile and mumbled an apology. Alice noted the brief air of tension between them and, feeling a bit awkward, turned towards the Gothic again. She strained to look through the slit in between the two doors. The small gap didn't give much of a view, but she could just make out some of the interior marble walls coated with patches of mould and mildew. There were some old church pews resting against each other like fallen dominoes and no sign of the church having been used for some time.

'It's haunted, you know,' Ting stated matter-of-factly.

'What?' Alice jerked her head out of the opening.

'The ghost of a murdered nun haunts the tower,' Ting casually added.

Alice looked in horror. 'A murdered nun?' She conjured up an image of Sister Martin with her shotgun.

Felicity hunched herself over, imitating an old women and putting on a strained, broken voice 'The old people tell of a tale most horrendous and vile. That of a nun murdered and thrown from the top of the tower to land on that very spot.'

She pointed at a place beyond Alice's feet. Alice saw through the joke and laughed.

'Seriously though,' Ting interrupted, 'the seniors say it *is* haunted. There is a crypt under the church where they buried the first of the old nuns who died after fleeing Ypres. And there is a girl buried in the cemetery with the other nuns. *I* haven't ever heard anything, but I suppose it is the perfect place to hang out at night if you are a ghost.' Ting smiled at the other girls.

'Hang on a second.' Alice put up her hand to pause Ting. 'What do you mean there is a girl buried?'

'Yeah, see the stone cross over there.' Ting pointed over towards a small cemetery. Alice jumped down the few steps from the Gothic entrance and followed to where Mary-Jane now stood near a fence. Alice took in the neat, tidy space. It was a very simple cemetery, well kept with a few small black crosses in rows surrounded by the wrought-iron fence that the girls now leant against. In the far corner standing out from all the simple black crosses of the nuns stood a stone Celtic cross. From where she stood, Alice couldn't make out the writing on the cross.

'Who was she?' Alice asked.

'She was a student killed from a hockey ball and buried here because she loved Kylemore,' Mary-Jane quickly explained.

'I heard she broke her neck falling off the mountain,' Felicity corrected.

Alice looked to Ting, judging she would have an answer. Ting shrugged her shoulders. 'There are all sorts of stories about her. The seniors get a great thrill out of trying to spook the juniors with ghost stories and warnings about sneaking out at night, or walking the grounds. All scare tactics, I think.'

'Maybe she was killed by a falling murdered nun?' Alice

giggled. Felicity laughed at Alice's new twist on the ghost story. Mary-Jane crossed her arms indignantly.

A sudden movement in the bushes on the other side of the cemetery caught Alice's eye. She scanned its fringes, thinking she saw a shadow of someone. A small breeze blew, chilling her, and the branches swayed. The shadow was gone. Seeing the gate to the cemetery, Alice was tempted to go further and take a closer look at the stone cross, but was interrupted by Ting.

'We have to get back.' Ting tapped her wristwatch impatiently. 'Dame Mary will be wondering where we are and we have already missed most of first study'

'Boo-hoo,' Mary-Jane mocked. 'Ting has missed out on doing her homework.'

Ting bit her lip and kicked a pebble at her foot.

'Come on.' Felicity caught up with Ting. 'Whatever about study, Dame Mary will be wondering where we are.'

Alice had almost forgotten all about her parents and Dame Mary. She was fascinated with the story of the girl and the Gothic, but now was anxious to get back and find out whether or not she was to have a future at Kylemore.

Alice gazed around the cemetery and blinked a few times. Again she thought she sensed something, a disquiet that she couldn't put her finger on. Then she shrugged, dismissing it, and picked up the pace with Ting and the girls as they made their way back to the Abbey.

★★★

There was a lightness in Alice's step as she entered the library and crossed the room towards her parents. She couldn't help grinning, having convinced herself that she felt at home in Kylemore and with the girls that she had met so far.

Mary-Jane, Felicity and Ting followed behind Alice into the room, Felicity having pulled up her socks before entering. They took on an air of well-mannered young ladies as they greeted Dame Mary and Alice's parents.

'You had a nice walk, girls?' Dame Mary asked the ensemble before her.

'Yes, Dame Mary, we went to the Gothic and back,' Ting spoke for the group.

'Very good, thank you, girls. Would you like to take some brack with you before you go on up to study?'

The three girls stepped forward. A paper napkin was offered to each of them with cake, and they were dismissed with another thank you, but not before saying goodbye to Alice and her parents.

After the three girls had left the room, Dame Mary turned to Alice and offered her another slice of the home made fruit cake.

'No, thank you.'

'Are you sure? Most girls here would jump at the chance of extra cake.'

'Yes, Dame Mary, I'm sure, thank you.'

The nun smiled at Alice, her oversized front teeth poking over her lower lip, creating a slightly comical but endearing expression.

'I think Alice will get on very well here,' she declared, looking at Alice's parents.

There was a brief silence. Alice looked quizzically at her mother.

'Excuse me, Sister, I mean Dame Mary, but does that mean Alice has been accepted?' asked Alice's equally confused mother.

'Would you like that, Alice?' The nun directed her gaze at Alice.

'I'd like that very much, Dame Mary.' Alice's eyes sparkled.

'Then I think that settles it.' Dame Mary smiled and pushed her spectacles up the bridge of her nose.

Unable to help herself, Alice lunged forward, threw her arms around the rotund nun and felt quite at ease giving her a big hug of gratitude, much to the delight of Dame Mary and complete and utter surprise of Alice's parents.

CHAPTER 6

Letter of Acceptance

'What's that?' Alice pointed at the additional paper included in Alice's acceptance letter.

'It's a list of all the things you'll need for school.' Alice's mum didn't look up.

'Oh, can I see?' Alice strained to look over her mother's shoulder.

Alice's mum went to the kitchen table and sat down. It was a two-page list of everything from underwear to sports kits, from a needle basket to name tags.

'My, this is extensive,' Alice's mum sighed. 'I think you will need more than one bag by the time we're through getting you all this lot.' She handed the list to Alice.

Alice scanned through the detail.

'What do they mean by *indoor shoes*?' asked Alice.

'I suppose the girls must wear different shoes outdoors to those that they wear indoors, practical when you think about it. I could do with enforcing something similar here.' Alice's mum nodded towards the muddy footprints leading to where Alice now sat at the table.

'In the forest again, were you?' Alice's mum asked.

'Huh?' Alice wasn't paying attention, head down, engrossed in the rest of the list.

'Were you having fun in the forest?' Alice's mum asked seriously as she cleared her now cold coffee cup from the table.

Alice looked up from the list. 'Forest? Oh yeah. Pete and I are making a hideout for ourselves so we can spy on wild animals. Pete says there's definitely a fox and possibly a badger's trail there. I'm going to go early tomorrow to work on the hideout some more. Dad said we can take some of the old scrap wood. I am going to make a table for it.'

Alice's mum smiled. Alice knew her mum liked Pete, always fussing over him when he called round, and singing his praises when he wasn't. There had been a considerable gap between Alice and her older brother Michael and her sister Christine. Sometimes Alice's felt like an only child. Pete lived near by and came from a large family. There was a gap in his too and the two had been shoved together when their respective siblings used to hang out together. Alice didn't remember actually meeting Pete, he just always was part of her growing up. Always there. They were so very different, and yet so enjoyed each other's company.

'Do you think you'll miss Pete?' Alice's mum asked.

'Oh, he's coming too. Sure, he's the tracker, can easily spot an animal trail, and can tell the difference between badger and fox dung. No problem! Pete's crucial to the exhibition.'

Alice's mum smiled.

'No, sweetie, I mean will you miss Pete when you're at Kylemore?'

Alice paused and looked back at the list again. 'Nah, sure I'll have lots of new friends in Kylemore. Anyway, he'll be stuck in primary school for another year regardless of where I go. He'll have to make do with his own classmates for a change. I'll write to him often. Every week. And we'll see each other over the hols. He'll be grand.'

Alice was scanning the list absent-mindedly as she walked towards the door.

'I'm sure *he* will.' Alice's mum said, and added, 'by the way, I think you meant to say *expedition*.' But Alice had already deserted her.

CHAPTER 7

New Beginnings

The last couple of weeks of the summer passed slowly, but now she was packed and ready to go. Standing at the door to her bedroom, Alice glanced around as if for the last time and, with a sigh, dragged the last of her bags down the stairs to the hall and out to the car.

Alice had initially been upset when her parents told her that they would not be bringing her to school for her first day. They had gotten their dates mixed up, which was typical of them, and now that they had the two weeks' holiday booked and paid for, they couldn't cancel. They had made alternative arrangements for Alice's journey to boarding school. Anyway, they justified their actions with the fact that they had already been to the school with Alice, had met and liked Dame Mary, and didn't have any worries about Alice settling in. They had arranged for Mr and Mrs Johnson to bring her to school with all her bags, so it was not like she was having to make her own way there this time.

Mrs Johnson had been their housekeeper for years and Alice's parents often called on her when in need of babysitting or as a stand in for times when her parents couldn't make a ballet performance or school recital.

Alice shoved the last of her bags into the boot and jumped into the back seat.

'Ready to go?' Mrs Johnson asked, leaning back over the passenger seat.

'As ready as I will ever be, I suppose,' Alice replied and smiled at Mr Johnson watching her in the driver's mirror.

The journey to Kylemore was tedious. Endless. Alice

wished she could beam herself up there in a flash. Like in *Star Trek*. Mr and Mrs Johnson seemed to be enjoying themselves, having the luxury of her parents' Mercedes Benz to drive, and money for food, fuel and accommodation to boot. They had stopped twice for lunch and afternoon tea and again for fuel, and yet they were still not there.

Sleep helped Alice as far as Limerick, but her racing mind and the bad roads prevented her from nodding off a second time.

At last they were in Galway and heading out towards Clifden and finally took the turn off into the valley that led them on the long, lonely road to Kylemore. It was a bleak-looking land with little to no human activity save the odd car that passed them in the opposite direction. When they did eventually make it to the causeway revealing the castle and lake, Mr and Mrs Johnson had to pull in and take in its beauty. 'Gosh, now there is a picture of elegance,' said Mrs Johnson. Mr Johnson sucked in a long, high whistle.

Alice fidgeted in her seat. She was wide awake now and feeling nauseous with the excitement.

'Yes, yes, nice view,' Alice squirmed, 'can we just get there?'

The final moments of driving up the long tree-lined drive and up the parapet to the front door were over in an instant, and Alice found herself standing in a daze as Mr Johnson started to unload her bags.

'Well, I suppose we'd better go in and find someone, my dear.' Mrs Johnson took hold gently of Alice's hand and started towards the main door.

Feeling childish, Alice shook off Mrs Johnson's hand. There was some activity inside – Alice's eyes took in her surroundings, familiarising herself again with the interior of the great hall, unable to believe that six months had passed since her interview. Some older-looking girls were busy with their parents or hovering in small groups looking on at her arrival, and then Alice recognised a nun making her way towards them in the hallway.

'Welcome, I'm Sister Valentine,' and she extended a hand towards Mrs Johnson.

'Hello, Sister Valentine, this is Alice Stone, it's her first day today. Her mum and dad couldn't make the trip so we are dropping her off.'

'Ah yes, Alice. I remember you.' Sister Valentine appeared somewhat perplexed, frowning for a moment, but then welcomed Alice with a familiar forced smile and looked questioningly to Mrs Johnson.

'Oh, I am sorry, I am Mrs Johnson, their housekeeper and, I suppose, sort of caretaker for the Stones.' Mrs Johnson smiled affectionately at Alice. 'My husband is on his way in with Alice's bags.'

'Of course,' Sister Valentine said, adding 'it's just that we were not expecting Alice until tomorrow.'

Alice's stomach lurched; she looked to Mrs Johnson.

'Oh dear, we must have got the dates mixed up with your parents holidaying and all,' Mrs Johnson laughed. 'I'm sure that's not a problem for the school?' Mrs Johnson face turned serious as she looked Sister Valentine in the eye.

Sister Valentine stared, unspeaking, at both Alice and Mrs Johnson.

'No, of course not.' She forced another smile at Alice.

Alice didn't know where to look.

'Well, I suppose that is it then, Alice,' Mrs Johnson declared, and Alice found herself getting a big hug and kiss. Mr Johnson hung back behind them, standing with the bags at his feet and not relinquishing his role of minder just yet.

'Best of luck, Alice.' He stepped in and ruffled her hair. 'Be good,' and with a wink he turned and started for the door. Alice looked on, bewildered that this was it, and that they were actually going. She stood silent for a moment and looked to Sister Valentine.

'Right, Miss Stone. Let's get you settled in. You are the first of the first years to arrive, and as we were not expecting you until tomorrow, I will get one of the seniors to show you up to the dorm and find your cubicle. Don't worry about your bags for now, I will arrange for Ben, our handyman, to bring them up for you shortly.'

Feeling the blood rush to her cheeks, Alice felt very foolish and rather peeved at her parents for getting it so wrong. Looking everywhere else except at the nun, Alice followed Sister Valentine as she made her way further into the hall. She looked up when Sister Valentine called out to an older looking girl in uniform.

'Alice, this is Megan. The exam years arrive early to settle in ahead of the other girls and to help with new arrivals.' Alice smiled meekly at her. Megan nodded at Alice. 'Megan, would you be so kind as to show Alice up to the big dorm? Perhaps introduce her to some of the other girls. You might even give her a brief tour so that she can get her bearings. Alice has arrived a day early, no doubt she will be a bit lonely for her class this evening. I know you will keep an eye on her.' Sister Valentine smiled stiffly at Alice and left.

Alice stood for a moment before Megan turned and quickly brought her in step with a commanding, 'Well, come on then.' Alice's stomach knotted. She wasn't feeling so welcome now.

Megan held open a door with a sign saying 'Private' on it and waved Alice through.

'So, you arrived a day early. Who got the dates messed up in your family then?'

Alice cringed. Then felt suddenly protective of her family.

'Oh that was no mistake. I thought it would be nice to arrive a day early, settle in before the others arrive.'

Megan paused and looked at Alice. 'Is that right? Gosh, you were keen. What did you say your name was again?'

'Alice, but you can call me Billy.' Alice thought this was as good a time as any to introduce her newly chosen name. Megan smiled.

'I see. Right, so Alice-call-me-Billy, come along then and we will find out where you are sleeping.'

Alice cringed. 'No, it's just Billy.'

Megan smiled. 'Okay, Just Billy. Come on and I'll show you around.'

Alice huffed, feeling a bit stupid.

The girls made their way up some steps from the hall and Alice found herself in a corridor where there was a large wooden boxed structure placed in the corner. Alice thought it looked like a confessional box and wondered what it was doing in the hall when Megan pointed at it.

'That is the telephone box.' She walked over and opened the door. Alice peered inside and saw a bulky black public phone set up on the wall with a strange turn handle attached to it.

'We are still a bit behind the times here, I'm afraid. This is one of the few dinosaur phones left. Our number is simply "Kylemore 6". Nothing normal about this place. No series of digits like we all have at home. No, this involves a bit of work on our part.' Megan stepped into the box and pointed to the handle. 'Turning a few times will ring down to Betty at the post office – you know that pretty cottage near the main gate?' Alice nodded. 'She will connect you to whatever number you want in the *real* world. Betty will instruct you when to put your money in the "A" slot and will interrupt you if you are running low and if more money is needed. She uses an old switchboard with the wires and plugs and has to ring the other side to make the connection first. Be careful what you say on the phone. Betty is a sweetie and all that, but she can listen in on any call.'

'What is the button "B" for?' Alice asked.

'Oh, that is the button you press when Betty actually connects you with the other side.' Alice was a bit confused.

'Oh don't worry, with the queues to use the phone on a Sunday evening, someone will show you how to use it properly the first few times.'

Alice thought of her parents abroad on holiday. She wouldn't be making any call this Sunday and felt a lonely pang for home.

The two girls curved their way around the corridor, with several big wooden doors off it. Each had signs nailed on to them with various saints' names.

'What's with all the saints' names?' Alice asked.

'Oh all the classrooms and dorms are named after saints. I think it is a *bless-all-who-enter-here* kinda thing. That one is the language room, and here is the TV room.' Megan swung open each door briefly, offering Alice a quick glimpse before shutting the door again. They then went up and up a long, narrow winding staircase. It was very enclosed and dark until they rounded a corner and then there was a burst of light from a skylight above. Alice could make out a couple of landings off which there were some more closed doors, and then at the summit of their climb were the dorms.

'Those doors there are the sixth-year dorms.' Megan pointed to the two other doors off the half landings. 'This one here is the Big Dorm where all the other Abbeyers live.' Megan pushed in the door. 'This was where the castle bedrooms were in the old days. Doesn't quite have the same *finesse* though.'

Alice found herself in a huge room with rows of cubicles all linked together. They had curtains for doors and the walls didn't quite make it up to the ceiling. She imagined she was like a mouse in a labyrinth, with some mad scientist looking down on her.

Megan was looking at a cubicle plan pinned up on the door. 'Can't see any *Just Billy* here.' She smirked at Alice and went to the end of the list. 'Never mind getting the wrong day, are you sure you haven't got the wrong school as well?'

Alice panicked inwardly. She felt foolish and a small fire of anger rose in the pit of her stomach. She was about to say something when Megan interrupted her.

'Ah, here you are.' Megan tapped a cubicle space somewhere on the chart and turned into the dorm. Dire Straits' *Walk of Life* echoed from someone's ghetto blaster somewhere from within the room.

'You must know someone in high places,' Megan said over her shoulder at Alice as she strutted along. 'Not often that a first year gets a wall cubicle, let alone one with a window. Who did you pay off then?'

'What do you mean?' Alice didn't like where the conversation was going.

'First Years are at the bottom of the rung. Then it is any other new girl by rank of year, after that it's by seniority. The Head Girl gets top of the pick in the sixth-year dorm. Prefects and class reps are next. Then it is who is here the longest. Some girls get down to the nitty-gritty details of who arrived before whom and at what time! In the big dorm there is a great demand for the cubicles on the walls with windows. They are usually first nabbed by prefects and seniors. Unless Miss Ash, the supervisor, has a soft spot for you. There are only so many windows after all.'

Alice didn't know what to say. She was secretly delighted

but puzzled as to how her name got onto a prized cubicle. 'Perhaps it is a mistake,' Alice offered with a meek smile.

'Won't be long and you will find out. Come on and we'll take a look at your space.' The cubicles were miserable looking with a bare bed and mattress and poster-less walls. And then there were one or two where someone had already unpacked and given their own personal touch to the cubicle with themed bedding, cool posters and family photos, transforming the space into a personal retreat.

Megan stopped at a cubicle, and Alice bumped into her.

'Well, here you are.'

Alice couldn't see what all the fuss was about. It didn't look much bigger than the other cubicles. There *was* a window and a solid wall at one end, but there was still the clammy looking single bed, the industrial sink and barren chest of drawers. Her curtain was a garish paisley-patterned orange and green colour that didn't even go all the way to the floor. She looked indignantly at Megan.

'Not very exciting, I know, but give yourself a few years here and it is all the small details that are important,' Megan laughed.

Alice walked into the cubicle and looked out the window. There was nothing to see but solid damp rock that climbed sharply skyward.

'Won't get much of a view from there,' Megan said. 'You are looking at the back of the mountain, my friend. The castle is built into it. A few years ago some girls used to sneak out the windows and down the mountain but they have since been nailed. The windows that is, not the girls! Put an end to that form of escape at least.' Megan smiled crookedly at Alice. 'The windows on the other side are the ones with great views. Only prefects get those. There would be holy war if you were to have got one of those.'

Alice was tempted to test the window herself but, on seeing Megan turn and leave, thought she would have plenty of time to try that out again and quickly caught up with her.

'So, do you want to meet some of the Sixth Years and see how the better half live?'

Megan headed out of the Big Dorm, down the stairs to the half landing and stopped outside a closed door with a big sign saying, 'Knock, or suffer the consequences'. Megan, ignoring the sign, stormed in.

'Hidey-hi, anyone home?' Megan shouted out over a blaring David Bowie's *Star Man*. Alice quickly took in the small L-shaped room that housed a small number of cubicles. There was a corner that she could not see beyond. Somewhere from within a deep booming voice replied, 'Hey-up!'

'Hey, Carrie, come and meet my new pet tag-along.' Megan smiled at Alice.

Alice heard the swish of a curtain being rapidly drawn back and then a tall bulky form stepped out. Alice was caught for breath at the presence before her. The girl stood giant-like with broad shoulders and a Mohawk hairstyle. She was in uniform, just about, with a mid-thigh smock dress and an oversized navy cardigan that still didn't hide her large frame.

'Carrie La-Bouche, meet Just Billy. Just Billy, officially known as Alice, this is Carrie.' Carrie raised an eyebrow quizzically at Megan. 'Fresh start and all that,' Megan offered jokingly as an explanation.

Alice squirmed and smiled shyly at Carrie who nodded understandingly. Megan then went on to detail Carrie's position in rank.

'Carrie is Head Girl, captain and goalie for our school's senior hockey team and first in the queue for whatever she wants to queue for. You don't mess with La Bouche!'

Carrie gave two fingers to Megan, smiling as she did.

'So, *Just Billy*, what has you here today? Thought the first years weren't coming till tomorrow?'

Alice looked at Megan and confessed.

'Yeah, we got the dates messed up.' Alice stared at her feet.

'Hey, lucky you, you get to spend your first night with us seniors,' and she thumped Alice on the back, making her stumble. 'You find your cubicle?' Carrie made her way over to a small kitchenette and filled a kettle.

'She's got a window,' Megan bragged for Alice.

Carrie turned and looked to Megan. 'Really?' She looked at Alice and gave a long slow whistle.

'So who do you know in high places?'

'Yup, that's what *I* said.' Megan went over and got herself a mug. 'Tea?' She waved the mug to Alice.

'No thanks.' Alice was worried now, and puzzled over all their talk of people in high places.

Carrie took the mug from Megan. 'You might as well have a cuppa, come tomorrow you won't be setting foot beyond that threshold, let alone getting an offer of a cup of tea.' She threw a teabag into the mug. 'A window, now that *is* something special. Did you tell Just Billy here about our Little Miss Someone?' Carrie was looking at Alice, but the question was directed at Megan.

'No.' Megan picked a bit of fluff off her jumper.

'Yeah, suppose you're right. Wouldn't want her getting upset on her first night, would we?' and without looking at Alice she poured the hot water into the mug.

CHAPTER 8

Wandering

By the time Alice arrived back, she found her bags waiting for her at the entrance to the Big Dorm and dragged them down to her cubicle. She had unpacked and put away her things neatly and was sitting on her bed thinking how pathetic her bare walls looked. She regretted now not buying some posters and not bringing more photos with her. Then she wondered what Pete was up to back at home. She looked at her watch and realised that it was only five o'clock, that it would be another while before she would be called by Megan for supper. She quickly forgot about Pete and got to thinking about this Miss Someone that Megan and Carrie had referred to. No doubt she would soon find out as more of the students arrived. For now it seemed only Sixth Years and a few of the foreign girls were in the school. Those that she had seen earlier seemed to have disappeared into their own cubicles. And judging from the silence behind the closed curtains, Alice guessed they were recovering from jet-lag and catching up on some sleep before supper.

With some time to kill, Alice thought of going back down to the lower dorm and made her way onto the landing when, feeling brave, she decided to explore a bit and have a look around for herself. There were, after all, only two flights of stairs to consider – the one she had already come up and the other that Megan had explained led to the Refectory and the classrooms. Alice decided to head towards the classrooms.

The stairway was steep and led away from light down into darkness. Alice found her eyes having to adjust as she descended, and fought an urge to return to the Big Dorm. She was, after all, starting afresh and needed to prove to herself that she was brave and independent enough to do some simple exploring. Reasoning that this could not be any worse than the first time she explored the woods below her own house, Alice carried on. But the stairs soon led into a series of corridors and doors, some that led into empty classrooms and others that led to yet another maze of corridors and even more doors.

Alice was beginning to feel confused and uncomfortable and was worried that she was getting lost. She regretted leaving the security of her cubicle. Moving along, round a bend, she found herself standing before a peculiar looking arched door that stood at the end of the quiet corridor. It was small and narrow, built into an arch in the wall. It looked medieval with its metal hinges and quaint shape. Waiting a moment, Alice listened to the stillness around her and then gave the round handle a pull.

The door opened stiffly, and she had to give it an extra tug to pull it fully open. Alice recoiled at the wall of damp, musty air that hit her. And then was pleasantly surprised to discover an old metal spiral staircase that coiled around up into a tower.

She checked over her shoulder and, hearing nothing, paused briefly before climbing up the steps.

The tower was narrow, with the staircase winding upward in an anti-clockwise direction. The walls were caked in a damp flaky whitewash, and the paint of the staircase patchily covered the tired old decorated metal beneath. Angled shafts of sunlight sliced into the tower at intervals through narrow gothic-like windows.

As she climbed, Alice caught narrow framed images of the lake and mountain beyond through the windows. At the top of the stairs was a second door, similar to the one below. She had to force it inwards to open it. She found herself in a small room strewn with old cases and bags and with tall, dust-encrusted windows on the opposite side of the room.

Much to Alice's surprise there was a girl sitting on the window ledge looking out. She turned her head and looked at Alice.

'Oh, I'm sorry. I didn't realise there was someone here,' Alice said, feeling a bit awkward. And then Alice thought she recognised the girl as the one she saw on the day of the interview. 'Oh, it's you, I think I saw you here when I came for my interview. That was you, wasn't it?'

The girl stared at Alice with wide open eyes. Feeling rather uncomfortable, Alice figured they both were somewhere they shouldn't be. Hurriedly, she turned to leave. 'I'm sorry, I'll go'.

'No, wait,' the girl called after her. 'Please. Don't go.'

Alice stopped and watched as the girl made her way off the ledge. She was petite and very pale. Alice figured she was similar in age to herself but there was something about her that Alice couldn't quite put her finger on, and then in a moment realised what it was. The girl was dressed in a grey school uniform but it seemed strangely old-fashioned. Her tunic was similar to that which Carrie had worn but this girl's was of another time, like it had a Charleston twenties look about it. Her hair was a short bob with a wide black satin hairband tied in a bow behind her ear. She looked like someone dressed for a fancy dress party.

The girl moved slowly towards Alice.

'I'm Alice. I arrived a day early, the rest of the First Years aren't coming till tomorrow,' Alice blabbered nervously. She figured the girl to be a junior by her size, but there was something in the depth of her eyes that made Alice think her much older.

'I'm Ruth,' the girl said unblinkingly. She hesitated, and then asked, 'You can see me?'

'Huh?' Alice thought it was rather stupid question to be asking.

All of a sudden the girl was standing right in front of Alice. Alice suddenly felt claustrophobic. Now that the girl was closer, Alice could see that her eyes were very dark, so dark that Alice thought that her irises and pupils were one.

'I'm sorry . . . I didn't mean . . . It's just . . . well before now I've never been seen by anyone.' The girl spoke hesitantly.

Feeling a creeping discomfort come over her, Alice's senses were on alert. Frozen and unmoving, Alice's eyes darted towards the door looking to escape.

Ruth smiled and burst into animated chatter. 'Gosh you have no idea how fantastic this is. It's been *so* long and despite a lot, and I mean *A lot* of effort on my part, I have never managed to get anyone to see me. And then here you are just turning up in my old classroom and you talk to me as if I am just one of the girls.'

Alice couldn't move. It was as if her feet were a ton weight and stuck fast in a block of concrete.

Ruth looked at Alice's petrified face. 'Gosh, I am sorry. I'm not making much sense, am I?' She stepped back away from Alice.

Alice shook her head, staring at the girl before her.

'I suppose that's because I have been dead for so long,' Ruth giggled. She quickly went on to explain that she had died while at school and despite all her rehearsing for the moment of meeting someone, it was she that had been taken completely by surprise. She had recognised Alice from the day of her interview some time ago, and thought she caught Alice looking up at her, but had put it down to coincidence. And now here they were, and she was able to say hello like you might to a new neighbour. It was too fantastic.

'I am sorry, truly I am. Please don't be frightened. I won't hurt you. I couldn't.' At this Ruth stepped further away from the terrified Alice.

'It's just been so long since I have spoken with anyone, and I am so excited about you seeing me, you can't possibly imagine what this means for me.'

Alice blinked a few times. Finding her breath once again, she regained some composure and decided to try and say something.

'I . . . it's just that . . . I mean...Who . . ?' Alice paused, her heart thumping in her chest, her mouth feeling dry.

Ruth smiled gently at Alice.

'Are you . . . you're a ghost?' Alice finally managed.

'Well, I suppose I am. I am not alive, that is for sure. I know you can see me, but can you see all of me?'

Alice found Ruth's question rather odd and was surprised to hear herself laugh.

'Well, you're not headless, if that's what you mean!'

Ruth giggled and put her hand up to her mouth. She couldn't remember the last time she had giggled at someone else's joke.

'But what can you see? I mean *how* do you see me?'

'When was the last time you looked in a mirror?' Alice asked, and then added, 'Can you look in mirrors?'

'Oh I see reflections all right but never my own for some reason. Believe you me, I have tried. I have tried lots of things but to no avail. I don't have companion ghosts to advise and instruct me.'

'Oh, don't you?' Alice didn't know what a ghost might or might not have, but she certainly never thought one might be totally alone. Not in a place like Kylemore where there must be so much history, and lots of people after dying.

Ruth gave Alice a twirl, spinning around in a circle, holding out the skirt of her pinafore as she completed a perfect pirouette.

'So how *do* I look?' Ruth giggled.

Alice watched as Ruth twirled on the spot. She had an infectious laugh and Alice found it difficult to believe that Ruth was an actual ghost. She seemed more like a young girl who was happy to have a friend and to show off a newly bought dress. Alice found herself warming to her.

'You look very well . . . considering.' Alice beamed at Ruth, beginning to enjoy the game. 'Was that your school uniform?'

'Yes, I sometimes try to imagine other clothes I used to have, but this is what is strongest in my memory, and I suppose that is what helps when it comes to wearing something in my world.'

'Oh.' Alice didn't know what to say to that.

The two were interrupted by the ringing of a church bell. Alice froze and looked around her, trying to decide where the noise was coming from.

'That's the bell calling the nuns for Vespers,' Ruth explained.

Alice felt pulled back into reality and panicked that she might be missed. 'I'm sorry, Ruth, but I probably should be getting back, the seniors will be looking to take me to supper shortly.'

'Oh, of course,' Ruth pouted but then smiled. 'Hey, don't worry. Now that I know you can see me, I can visit you anytime. And I have all the time in the world. You go and have some supper and I will catch up with you later.' She escorted Alice to the top of the stairwell.

Alice wasn't sure what to make of the whole thing. Although the idea of seeing and knowing a friendly ghost seemed very exciting, she couldn't help feeling a bit worried about the idea of Ruth being able to seek her out wherever and whenever she chose. Alice stopped at the top of the stairs. 'Is this your place? I mean, can you leave here, the tower?'

'Yes, of course. Mind you, it would seem I can't go beyond the estate. Not that I would want to, not sure how to put it, but I kind of like it that way.'

Ruth's attention wandered.

Alice didn't like to think much about what she might mean and then realised something.

'Oh, hang on, are you the girl that was buried in the cemetery? And then added 'And no one has seen you till now?'

Ruth shook her head.

'Oh.' Alice thought for a moment. 'But why now, why me?'

'I am sure I don't know,' Ruth said. 'But I am so pleased you have found me, Alice. I think it is a good sign. No doubt we will be great friends.' She beamed a smile at Alice and disappeared through the wall.

CHAPTER 9

On Meeting Ruth

A bewildered Alice found her way back along the corridors and up the stairs back to her cubicle. She was a bit numbed by what had happened and sat staring blankly on her bed for some time. It wasn't long before Megan found her to take her to supper.

Alice didn't let on that she had already ventured downstairs toward the classrooms and was pleased to be led away from the tower to the Refectory, or Ref, as she would learn to call it. Alice couldn't quite believe what had taken place and was mulling it over in her head, but didn't know how to make sense of it. She knew it would sound crazy to tell anyone about Ruth, and anyway she probably would get into trouble for wandering off and going up the tower in the first place. She remembered that Dame Mary had made it quite clear the day of her interview that the towers were out of bounds.

'You're very quiet this evening,' Megan said, interrupting Alice's thoughts as they approached the Ref.

'Huh? Oh, sorry, it's just that I . . . I'm tired,' Alice mumbled.

'Yeah, that would make sense, you fitted in a lot today. Long old journey and then the trauma of starting here. Have a good supper and take it easy this evening, it'll be an even longer day tomorrow with the arrival of the rest of the First Years. You'll probably get a second wind after you get something to eat anyway.' Megan held open a door for Alice. 'Here we are.'

Alice was presented with a modern metal staircase that

dropped steeply, connecting the first floor with the ground floor. There was another closed door at the bottom of the stairs.

'Not very exciting, is it?' Megan teased. 'Come on – the Ref is just beyond the lower door.'

Alice pushed in the door and found herself in a large, tired-looking room. She guessed it must have once served as one of the main rooms of the castle. The room was as wide as it was tall and the ceiling was decorated with intricate details of roses and borders looking like exaggerated icing detail from a wedding cake. Large arched windows masked by plain net curtains gave a hazy view onto the parapet. Faded fanciful velvet wallpaper lined the walls. There was a huge black-marble fireplace boarded up and partially hidden by a large stainless-steel kitchen unit. A strong smell of egg and toast wafted through the air. And then to give it all the genuine stamp of being a real refectory, there were rows of tables and benches where great chaises longues and card tables might have once stood.

'Impressive, isn't it?' Megan asked the stunned Alice. 'It is nice to leave the hospital-like feel of the classroom corridors and dorm to come and dine here. Although, give yourself a few days of dining here and the food will do enough to burst any glamour bubble.'

'Where are we? I mean, what was it before?'

'Oh, not sure really, I think it used to be the lounge or drawing room.' Megan wasn't interested anymore; she had spotted the other seniors and was already on her way over to them. Alice had to hurry to catch up. All the other tables were unoccupied.

Alice smiled shyly as introductions were made to the other Sixth Years, and it wasn't long before she found herself blending into the background and just listening on as the older girls' banter took over from the confusing thoughts mulling around in her head. Talk of the holidays, who had done what and where, and gossip about others passed the time. After a fairly mediocre supper of scrambled eggs on soggy toast with a few slices of tomato on the side, the girls slowly made their way back upstairs happily chatting away with each other. Nobody was talking to Alice.

Megan saw Alice back into the Big Dorm and to her cubicle and, anxious to get back to her own friends, bid her goodnight.

'Miss Ash will be along shortly for lights out and you will be called for breakfast at eight in the morning. Keep on her good side. You don't want to mess with Ash. Try and sleep well.' Megan smiled sympathetically. 'You probably won't, being your first night, but that is to be expected.' With that Megan pulled shut Alice's cubicle curtains and left.

Alice got undressed and got into bed. She no sooner had settled under the duvet and was trying to get warm and comfortable when a movement caught her eye. She stifled a scream.

Ruth had appeared at her bedside, beaming a great big smile down at her. 'Don't worry, it's only me. Thought I would come and say goodnight.'

'Crikey, Ruth, you scared the life out of me,' Alice said loudly, then whispered, 'What are you doing here?'

'Sorry, I will have to try and make a better entrance next time.' She sat on the edge of Alice's bed. Alice instinctively jerked her knees up, clutching at her duvet, although she didn't actually feel any weight from Ruth.

'It's late, and I am really tired.' A nervous Alice pulled the duvet further up around her chin.

'Oh, I'm sorry, I thought we could talk before lights out. You don't mind, do you? It has been so long since I have had a conversation with anyone.' Ruth shuffled about a bit as if to make herself more comfortable.

Alice peered at her over her knees. Ignorant of Alice's discomfort and the effect her presence was having on her, Ruth chatted on. 'This is so great. You have no idea what this means to me. In fact, I am not so sure I understand it myself. I mean, why is it that only you see me, and why now after all this time? But to be honest, I am just so excited about having someone to talk to. I can hardly believe it myself.'

'Well, it is just a tad strange for me, too, you know.' Alice sat up in the bed. 'I mean, I'm not exactly in the habit of meeting ghosts and having conversations with them.'

'Oh, are you not?' Ruth sounded surprised.

'Did you think I was some sort of psychic or something and did this kind of thing all the time?

Ruth looked perplexed. 'I am sure I do not know what you are, but you can see me and hear me, and here we both are having a conversation. I thought perhaps you had some gift or something?'

'No,' Alice said indignantly. 'Maybe you are just a figment of my imagination, my mind gone into shock from having arrived in the middle of nowhere?'

Ruth giggled. 'I hope not, because if I am a figment of your imagination then I must be one of my own too, and that would make us both mad.'

Alice thought that one through and found herself smiling at Ruth.

'So you mean to say that you have never seen a ghost ever in your life before, never sensed one or experienced anything out of the ordinary?'

'No.'

'Nothing at all?'

'Unless you count those times when you, say, think of

a friend, and then suddenly that friend phones you, or like when you get this really odd feeling that you have been somewhere before when you get there, but haven't. I have a friend whose granny likes to talk to her dead husband, but I think that she is just a bit crazy.'

Ruth frowned and looked confusedly at Alice.

'Oh, never mind. No, I haven't, and I'm not sure what to make of all this.' Alice was about to ask Ruth a question when Ruth suddenly froze and put a finger up to her lips. 'Shush, here comes Miss Ash. She's not very friendly. Just play along with what she wants and you'll be fine.'

A voice roared from beyond the curtains.

'Lights out, girls, get into your own cubicles and no more talking.'

The steps stopped outside Alice's cubicle and suddenly the curtain was ripped back, exposing the bulky form of Miss Ash. Her cold grey eyes and thin-lined mouth sat limply in a round face that was framed by lank greasy bobbed hair. Alice thought she might be acceptable looking if she wore some makeup. She wore a heavy grey cord suit jacket over a matching skirt with bulletproof tights and brown laced-up mules.

Miss Ash scanned Alice's cubicle. 'Oh, I thought you had company.' Her double chins wobbled as she looked about her. She returned her focus to Alice. 'Ms Stone, I presume, I heard you decided to grace us with your presence a day early. Do you make it a usual habit of talking to yourself?' Miss Ash looked down her nose at Alice.

Alice felt unsure of what to say. She looked to where Ruth was sitting and back at Miss Ash. Ruth stuck out her tongue and pulled a face at Miss Ash. Pulling the duvet up around her mouth, Alice concealed a smile.

'Well, Miss Stone? Cat got your tongue?' Miss Ash asked impatiently.

'Oh, I am sorry, Miss Ash, I was . . . I was . . .' Alice looked to Ruth for inspiration. Ruth, sensing Alice's need, quickly clasped her hands together in prayer and looked up to the heavens.

'I'm sorry, Miss Ash, I was saying my prayers.'

'You were what? Oh, I see, right, I mean, of course. Good child. Well, just keep your prayers silent in future. You might get away with it tonight, but from tomorrow you will have to take into account all the other girls trying to get to sleep.' Miss Ash started to let the curtain slip shut and added finally, 'Breakfast is at eight thirty tomorrow.'

Miss Ash stepped back into the corridor and stopped for a moment to look back at Alice's cubicle, looking at the window and back to Alice. Glancing to each cubicle either side of Alice, Miss Ash looked as if she was about to say something, but did not. Making an effort of a smile, Miss Ash said goodnight and was gone.

'That was close. Thank you Ruth,' Alice whispered once she heard the steps fade down the corridor.

'That was fun. *Mizz* Ash is an old battleaxe who likes to take pleasure in making life difficult for the girls, especially the juniors. She is only ever pleasant when there is a nun around or if she needs something from you. Pulled the wool right over Dame Mary's eyes, she has. Gets away with too much, if you ask me. I've seen her up to her tricks with the girls and have not been able to do anything about it. I know that smile, she is up to something.'

Alice wasn't sure what that meant and didn't ask. Tiredness overcame her and, giving a big yawn, she slumped down in the bed. 'Ruth, I am so tired and I really want to go to sleep now. Can we talk again tomorrow?'

'Oh, all right then. You sleep well. I won't be too far away.'

Alice smiled sleepily and nodded before turning in towards

the wall of her cubicle. She had closed her eyes and let on she was relaxing into a sleep when her mind started to race over the events of the day. She glanced back over her shoulder to find herself alone once again. She wondered if she could always see Ruth if she was around, or did Ruth have the power to appear or disappear as she might like? Alice thought it might be easier if she could have some notion as to when Ruth was present. She certainly did not like the idea of Ruth being here now and not being able to see her. She turned her head back again towards her cubicle wall. Soon her thoughts turned to home, her mum and dad abroad, and Pete. What he would make of it, Alice would love to know. She imagined the letter she would not be able to write, knowing that he would never believe her, and mulled over who might. And then she remembered Pete's granny, Sally, who often spoke of the dead and teased them with stories about the 'other side'. Alice tossed and turned. She tired of counting sheep and resorted to attempting a decade of the Rosary before sleep finally found her.

CHAPTER 10

Arrival of a Certain Miss Someone

Alice was woken with a start as dormitory lights came on and the thundering voice of Miss Ash sounded the wake-up call. There were sounds of moans from other cubicles, and Alice found herself quite nervous and at the same time excited about the day ahead. She washed and got dressed quickly in her own clothes, as she had not been assigned any uniform yet, and then was undecided as to what to do next. Pulling back her curtain she glanced out, scanning the rest of the cubicles for movement and caught the eye of another girl.

'Hi there.' Alice made her way over to the girl as she started to make her way out of the dorm. 'Hey. Are you going to the Ref? Mind if I walk with you? My name is Billy, what's yours?'

'So I hear,' the girl answered in a heavy American accent, smirking at Alice. 'Hi *Alice*, I'm Tanya.'

Alice felt a bit foolish, wondering if the Billy idea was going to work. She decided to change the subject. 'You're American?'

'D'ya think?' Tanya answered sarcastically with an even heavier American drawl.

Alice smiled, embarrassed. 'What year are you?'

'Third.'

'I'm a First Year. I'm the first to arrive, the rest are due today. You arrived yesterday didn't you? I saw you when Megan brought me in. Did you travel far? I mean obviously from America but, like, do you have jet lag? Megan said you and whoever else was here had travelled far and would be jet-lagged. Where did you fly from? Are you still tired? I came from Cork yesterday, it took ages to get here and I was very tired but I cannot imagine what it must be like to fly across time zones. Is it weird?'

Tanya stopped walking and stared at Alice. 'Which question would you like me to answer first?' Without waiting for an answer, Tanya moved on.

Alice caught up with her and blabbered on nervously until they were at the Ref. Once there, Alice scanned the big room for Megan and Carrie. There were some of the other seniors filling a table but they were not familiar faces to Alice, so she went to sit with Tanya. Tanya glanced up at Alice

'Look, kid, just so you know. We may be having breakfast together now, but that's it, okay. As soon as some of your own class arrive you are on your own. First Years have their own table over there with the rest of the juniors.' Tanya pointed at a group of empty tables at the other end of the room. 'This is for Third Years, and that does not include you.'

Alice didn't know where to look. She mumbled an apology and, having lost her appetite for breakfast, went through the routine of taking some cereal and milk and pushing her cornflakes around with her spoon. She was just about to leave the table when there was a sudden movement and all the girls stood to attention. Dame Mary had entered the room, and a respectful silence followed in her wake.

'Good morning, girls.'

'Good morning, Dame Mary,' the girls responded in unison.

Dame Mary waved her hands, gesturing for the girls to sit down. 'Thank you, girls, please sit down and finish your breakfast.'

There was the sound of dragged benches as the girls settled themselves again. Alice was following Tanya's example and so remained standing as Dame Mary made her way towards their table.

'Good morning, Alice, Tanya, did you sleep well last night?'

'Yes, thank you, Dame Mary,' Alice joined Tanya's response.

'Tanya, I take it you have got over your jet lag after a good long sleep?'

'Yes, thank you, Dame Mary.'

'And how is your dear grandmother?'

'Grandmother is very well, she sends her best.'

Dame Mary looked to Alice. 'Tanya's grandmother was in school with me, oh I suppose it is a few years ago now.' The Dame smiled warmly at the two girls. 'We go back a long way. Tanya here is following in her grandmother's footsteps, aren't you Tanya?' Dame Mary beamed a smile at Tanya who smiled meekly back.

'And Alice, it was a pleasant surprise to find you here a day early. Did you use the opportunity to settle in for yourself?'

'Ah, yes Dame Mary.'

'It is a shame that there were none of your own class here, but I hope that with the help of Tanya and the other seniors you settled in nicely?'

Alice looked to Tanya, not sure how she fitted into the picture, but Alice was happy to agree. Alice thought of her encounter with Ruth and wondered should she ask for some private time with Dame Mary, but suddenly felt very shy.

'Well, you will be pleased to hear that the rest of your class are due to arrive today,' Dame Mary continued. 'So if you would like to go back to your cubicle and freshen up after breakfast you can come down to the lobby to Sister Valentine. Some of the other girls are arriving already, despite the early hour. I thought you might like to be there to meet and greet them as they arrive.'

'Yes, Dame Mary,' Alice nodded.

'I will be down myself shortly. Finish your breakfast and I will catch up with you in a little while.' Tucking her hands under her habit, Dame Mary nodded at the girls and slowly made her way over towards the Sixth Year table, chatting with them amicably.

Alice turned back to her now soggy breakfast. Excited about the prospect of meeting her classmates, she cleared her place, left the Ref and made her way up towards the dorm. Her head was full of thoughts of meeting her class mates when she jumped up the step into the Big Dorm and straight into another girl. The girl had been standing checking the list of names and assigned cubicles pinned to the dorm door when Alice barged into her.

'Hey, watch where you are going.' The girl shoved Alice back. She had long coiffed red hair and might have been pretty, but her air of intolerance made her features sharp and unattractive.

'Oh, I'm sorry, didn't see you there.' Alice stood back from the girl who was looking down her nose at Alice with a deep frown and a scornful face.

'Yeah, well you'd better get some eyes in your ugly face then, hadn't you?' The girl gave Alice a vicious look and then turned her attention back to the list. Alice was about to say something when Megan came past the two girls on the landing.

'Hey, looks like a Certain Miss Someone is being her usual friendly self.' Megan gave Alice a wink and passed on. Head down, Alice mumbled her apologies and escaped to her cubicle. Much to her relief, Alice found Ruth waiting for her.

'Ruth, am I glad to see you ... the girl with the red hair .. .' Alice didn't get a chance to finish when the cubicle curtain was yanked back.

'You! Who the hell do you think you are? This is *my* cubicle. *I* booked it last year. Get out!' It was the girl Alice had bumped into at the dorm door.

Alice stood, mouth open. Suddenly the girl grabbed at Alice's duvet and started to pull it off. Alice stared at her in disbelief. 'What are you doing? Stop. I'm sorry but . . .' Alice grabbed her duvet back and a tug of war started.

'You have no right to be here. Who the hell said you could move in here? This is mine. You're a First Year. Take your crap and get the hell out of here.' The girl let go of the duvet, causing Alice to fall backwards and land in the corridor with a thump. The raging red-head moved quickly into the cubicle and to the chest of drawers, where she yanked the top drawer open and started to throw the contents out into the central corridor at Alice.

Alice, still sitting on the ground, gaped in horror as all her personal stuff was thrown about.

'Stop! What is wrong with you? Please. STOP!' Tears began to well up, and a lump of anger wedged in her throat. She looked to Ruth, eyes pleading for her to do something.

In an instant there was a scream as the girl stood now with her hand caught in a closed drawer. She cried owut in a combined rage of pain and anger as she tried to pull her hand free. The drawer was wedged shut and she couldn't pull her hand out. Of course, Alice could see Ruth standing there, leaning fully on the drawer, preventing the raging red head from opening it. To anyone else it was as if the drawer had jammed shut.

'Stop struggling, will you? If you stop a minute, I'm sure the drawer will loosen.' Alice, standing now, glared at Ruth. Ruth moved aside and Alice stepped in and pulled the drawer open. The girl was sobbing, clutching her hand to herself, staring with wet eyes of hatred at Alice.

'What is going on here?'

Alice turned to see Miss Ash standing enormous looking, scowling at the scene before her.

'Oh, Miss Ash, I am so glad you came along. Alice here just lost it. One minute I am introducing myself to her and the next thing she is having a mad fit.' The girl sobbed and clutched her hand closer to her chest.

'What? That's not true.' Alice stared at the girl and back at Miss Ash.

'Your turn will come, Alice, let Alexandra finish.' Miss Ash put her hand up to stop Alice talking and looked softly at Alexandra. 'Tell me what happened, Alexandra.'

'Alice seemed to think I wanted to take her cubicle. I was joking with her about the list and the confusion of cubicle allotment and she started to have a fit, throwing all her stuff about the place. I was trying to put her things back saying it was okay, when she jammed the drawer on my hand.' At this Alexandra extended her red hand out for Miss Ash to inspect.

Miss Ash sucked in a breath of concern. 'My dear, that does look painful. What have you got to say for yourself, Miss Stone?'

Alice was flabbergasted. 'She's lying! I never . . .' Alice pointed at Alexandra. 'It was *her* that came demanding that I get out of the cubicle and started to throw all my things about.' Miss Ash crossed her arms and raised her eyebrows questioningly at Alice.

'Why would I throw all my own stuff about the place?' The tears flowed down her cheeks.

'Why indeed, Miss Stone? Why indeed? And tell me, Miss Stone, did Alexandra decide to go and jam her own hand in your chest of drawers all by herself?'

Alice was stuck for words. She looked to Ruth, who shrugged her shoulders apologetically. 'No . . . I mean, yes . . .

I mean.' Alice was confusing herself, not knowing what to say.

Alexandra walked towards Miss Ash. 'Miss Ash, I'm okay, it was just a bit of a shock really. I am sure Alice here is just a bit out of sorts, you know being so young and new. It is probably her first time away from home . . .' And here she whispered, 'probably another girl not wanted around by her parents.' And then more loudly, 'I am sure there was just some confusion in the list. Alice can have my cubicle if she prefers, I don't mind. Honestly.' Alexandra smiled a pitiful smile at Miss Ash.

'That is very decent of you, Alexandra. Decent, but unnecessary. We can't have girls taking cubicles willy-nilly. Think of the chaos it would cause. That is why there is a list. Now, I think Sister Josetta should take a look at your hand and, in the meantime, I will have a chat with Miss Stone here and sort out this cubicle confusion once and for all.'

'If you say so, Miss Ash.' Alexandra left to go but not before giving Alice a close-lipped victorious smirk behind Miss Ash's back. Alice felt a deep anger rise in her, knowing that this was not over.

'Right, Miss Stone, first of all you can pick up all these things and tidy up the cubicle. There has, indeed, been some confusion here and I want to get to the bottom of it. Do not leave the cubicle. I will be back very shortly.' Turning from the girls, Miss Ash found herself facing a small group of other students peering out of their curtains watching the scene. 'Mind your own business, girls,' Miss Ash ordered. And the curtains instantly dropped back into place.

Miss Ash turned and stormed away towards the doorway. Once gone, Alice pulled her own curtain closed and turned to Ruth and whispered angrily, 'I can't believe Miss Ash took her word over mine. What is Alexandra's problem? She is SUCH a liar.'

'Those two have a history.' Ruth shook her head as she

explained. 'Alexandra can't do anything wrong as far as Miss Ash is concerned. Sorry about the hand thing, wasn't thinking of Alex coming up with that excuse. Took some serious effort on my part to keep it closed. I don't have a whole lot of strength. Never had to do that before'

Alice moved slowly, picking up her clothes and her bed covers when Miss Ash arrived back with a copy of the dorm list in her hand.

'Right, Miss Stone, it would appear that there has indeed been some confusion about who got what. This is a copy of the original plan that I had signed off by Dame Mary, and it is quite clear that Alexandra, Miss Store, was originally assigned this cubicle. It is obvious someone did not read the list correctly and mixed up your names. A Stone for A Store. Easily enough done, I suppose. First Years are rarely assigned a cubicle with a window. I am surprised no one said as much. You have a temper that is unacceptable, Alice Stone. You will have to keep that at bay. We do not tolerate bad tempers here. I suggest you pack up your things and move your belongings to the cubicle you were originally assigned.' Miss Ash pointed to an unoccupied centre aisle cubicle. 'I will go and check on Alexandra, and will let her know that *her* cubicle is now available. Consider yourself warned, Miss Stone. One more antic like that and you will find yourself with detention and going to Dame Mary's office.' Miss Ash turned on her heel and walked away.

Alice slumped onto the bed and stared at Ruth. 'What a mess to get into. This is not how I envisaged my first day would be.' Ruth nodded and watched as Alice pulled her bags out from under her bed and started to re-pack her belongings, huffing and mumbling angrily at the world.

New Friends

When Alice eventually made her way down to the hall, after dumping her bags and her hastily packed belongings in her newly assigned cubicle, Dame Mary was already there. The big hall was full of noise now. Small clusters of excited girls and polite parents were pocketed here and there. There was a man, casually dressed in worn workers clothes, lugging bags and cases towards the dorms. Alice recognised him as Ben, who had brought her bags up the day before, and smiled politely at him as she neared him. He had a pleasant face, with bright eyes and, despite his hardened skin from working in all weathers, a friendly disposition. He gave her a nod and a humorous wink.

Most of the girls looked happy, but there were some who had a more raw and fresh look about them. Alice's eye was drawn towards a girl that stood apart from any of the chatting circles. She was wearing a bright berry-red, velvet high-buttoned coat and had beautiful long blond hair that hung loosely over her shoulders. The girl stood quietly, almost statuesque, her only movement being her eyes that took in the hall about her and her surroundings. Alice caught her eye and smiled, but the girl continued to stare as Alice made her way over towards her. Dame Mary stood nearby talking to a woman, both seemingly oblivious to the young girl who stood alone.

'Ah, Alice, good girl, here you are. Mrs Hughes, Gale, this is Alice whom I was telling you about. Alice, Gale will be in your class too, she is the first of the rest of your year to arrive today.'

'Hello.' Alice extended a hand towards Mrs Hughes. 'Pleased to meet you. Hi Gale.' Alice beamed a great big smile towards Gale and, feeling awkward about a handshake, raised her hand in a brief wave. 'I'm so glad there is another First Year here,' Alice said to break the ice. 'I arrived yesterday. A day early,' she added mocking herself.

Gale nodded politely at Alice, not saying anything, and looked towards her mother. 'Gale is very shy and doesn't say much, sure you don't, pet?' Mrs Hughes hugged her daughter tightly around her shoulders. Gale's expression didn't change. 'Unlike her mother, eh? Her mother does enough talking for the two of us, isn't that right, love?'

Another squeeze and expressionless response. Alice was about to ask Gale a question, but Mrs Hughes had already jumped in, filling the gap with, 'Ah yes, our Gale is very shy and quiet, Sometimes I have to check that she is still in the car with me, she can sit so still. Can make car journeys very long altogether, can't it, love?' Gale didn't answer.

'I am sure it won't be long and Gale will settle in and make some very good friends.' Dame Mary had stepped forward. 'I am conscious of the journey ahead of you, Mrs Hughes, best to say goodbye now. Alice here can show Gale her way to the dorm and help her settle in. Ben will drop your bags up to the dorm for you shortly.' Mrs Hughes glanced over at Ben as he disappeared up the stairs with another set of bags. 'Ben's family have worked on the estate for years,' Dame Mary said. And following Mrs Hughes's watchful eye, added, 'He's a good man and a hard worker.'

'Oh, yes, right.' Mrs Hughes drew her attention back to the girls when she realised that this was her goodbye moment. She hadn't quite prepared herself for it. There was the sudden sweep of arms and gush of last-minute affections. Alice felt awkward and couldn't help but feel embarrassed for

Gale as her mother burst into tears. Fortunately for them all, Dame Mary quickly came to the rescue, encouraging Alice and Gale on their way towards the dormitory while leading the distraught Mrs Hughes towards the exit.

The two girls were about to leave the now crowded hallway when some high-pitched squeals of joy stopped them and they turned to see the cause. Alice spotted a young girl lagging behind some new arrivals, struggling with a heavy bag and trailing trench coat. Hoping she was another First Year, Alice grabbed Gale by the arm and dragged her towards the new arrival.

'Hi there, are you a new First Year too?' Alice asked.

The girl smiled, brightening her otherwise plain features and revealing beautiful white teeth. 'Yeah, I'm Bessie, that's my sister, Ava, she's in Fourth Year. What's your name?'

'My name is Alice, but you can call me Billy.'

Bessie looked to Gale and laughed. Gale shrugged her shoulders.

'What? What's wrong with the name Billy anyway?' Alice asked indignantly.

'Oh nothing I'm sure, other than it being a boys' name, but I can't see anything wrong with Alice, I think it's a nice name. Better than Bessie anyway.' Alice didn't think there was anything wrong with the name Bessie but didn't comment. She looked to Gale.

'Hey, chin up, my mother's name is Storm. Try and live up to that.'

Alice looked at Bessie and back to Gale, she didn't quite get it at first and then a slow realisation dawned on her. Storm. Gale. Alice and Bessie giggled.

CHAPTER 12

Imaginary Friends

The girls found their cubicles, Alice having dou-ble-checked they took the right ones. It was a busy hive of girls chatting and unpacking, the cubicles gradually filling and the noise level rising as the morning progressed.

It wasn't long before Bessie and Gale sought out Alice and settled themselves on her bed for a chat. Alice thought it was nice hanging with the girls in the cubicle. She pre-ferred her own cubicle, which was that little bit more home-ly compared to Bessie's. Bessie had literally thrown her bags up onto her bed before tossing out their contents and then stuffed everything into the drawers. Alice had taken one look at the heap on Bessie's bed and decided she wouldn't hang around there. Gale, on the other hand, had not only unpacked everything meticulously but also had already made up her bed with matching duvet cover and pillow slip and had me-mentoes from home neatly placed on her countertop. There was a selection of fancy hair products, a very nice looking old-fashioned hairbrush and a large silver framed photograph of Gale's mother in a striking pose, signed '*To my darling Gale, missing you already, Mummy*'.

'Wow,' Bessie had said.

'Don't bother,' Gale had replied. 'She's an actress. Lives her whole life like she is always on stage.' Bessie and Alice looked at each other. Gale had then stepped out of her own cubi-cle, held the curtain back in an invitation to leave, then made her way over to Alice's cubicle. Alice and Bessie followed. All three were sitting comfortably there now.

Alice, having been the first to arrive, felt quite confident.

She happily bragged about her previous evening dining with the Sixth Years and being in their dorm. She took great pleasure in warning the others about Miss Ash and the Certain Miss Someone, but did not mention anything about Ruth. Alice wondered where Ruth might be hanging out. She hadn't seen any sign of her all morning

'So you were demoted on your first day?' Gale teased. 'What are the chances of that?'

'I don't know. I just went along with Megan, didn't really get much of a look at the actual list myself.'

'I suppose it would be easy enough to get the names mixed up. A Stone, A Store. They kinda would look the same at a quick glance,' Bessie offered.

'I should have copped on to something being wrong when Megan went on about the window. Anyway, it's sorted now and I don't plan on getting in Alexandra's way again anytime soon.' Alice played with the edge of her sock. 'I get a feeling that Alexandra is going to be trouble. And I bet you Miss Ash knew exactly who was supposed to be in that cubicle. I knew she was looking at it funny last night.'

Ruth suddenly appeared on Alice's countertop. She sat comfortable with her two legs dangling, listening intently at the ensemble before her. Alice's eyes kept moving to the place where Ruth now sat as she tried to continue on as normal. 'You will have to watch out for those two, Alice – I think Miss Ash and Alexandra will be trouble for you,' Ruth said aloud to Alice. Alice looked at Ruth and back to Bessie and Gale. She knew they were not able to see Ruth at all, but was still finding it very difficult to remain composed and not bothered that there was a ghost sitting up on her countertop.

Alice glared at Ruth and got up. 'I need to pee, back in a minute.'

'What are you at?' Alice demanded when Ruth appeared

at her side as she walked into the washroom. Alice's eyes scanned the entrance, nervous of someone coming in and finding her talking to herself.

'What did I do?' Ruth pouted.

'You can't just appear like that and start talking to me in front of others,' Alice whispered.

'Oh, Alice, I have been cooped up here with no one for company and just wanted to join in on your circle.' Ruth added, 'Bessie and Gale seem nice. Bessie is real bubbly and don't you just love Gale's hair. Mine doesn't grow any more.' Ruth patted her own short locks.

Alice ignored her. 'Look, Ruth, while I think it is really great meeting you and, well, I suppose just a tad weird, we are going to have to come up with some arrangement of when and how you, well, appear. I can't have you messing about in front of me when no one else can see you.' Alice folded her arms defiantly.

'This is new for me, too, you know.' Ruth stood, her shoulders hunched. 'I mean I don't want to spoil things for you, but look at it from my point of view. You get to chat with your new friends whenever you want. I haven't had a friend in so long, and now you're saying I have to make an appointment to see you?' Ruth huffed.

'No, it's not like that, I'm sorry. It's just all so weird.' Alice rubbed her forehead. Alice walked over to the sinks and washed her hands, checking her image in the mirror. 'While the idea of having an invisible friend might be a bit of fun, it's also weird. People will think I am mad.' Alice spoke into the mirror.

'You can say that again.' Alice jumped with fright. Alexandra had stepped out from another doorway.

'Alexandra, I didn't see you there. Where did you come from?' Alice was mortified at being caught and wondered how much Alexandra had overheard. Ruth stood next to Alice and spoke gently into her ear. 'There is another access beyond the toilets. It leads to the art classroom and some old rooms. Some girls go there to sneak a cigarette. I bet you that's where this *Certain Miss Someone* was.'

Alexandra walked slowly over to Alice.

'None of your beeswax,' Alexandra sneered. She took a step closer. Alice could smell the pungent smoky fumes from her breath and resisted fanning the smell away. Glancing around Alice, and oblivious to Ruth, Alexandra flicked her hair. 'Aren't you a bit old to have an imaginary friend? Or were you saying your prayers, again?' Alexandra sneered triumphantly. Alice was shocked that Alexandra knew that.

'Fit for the mad house, I think.' Alexandra snorted, before turning on her heel and strutting out of the wash room.

Alice was stumped. 'Why didn't you warn me she was coming?' Ruth glared at Alice. 'Well it's not that I can see around corners, you know,' she said defensively.

'Oh, can't you? I thought that was something you ghosts could do?'

'No, and I don't come with rattling chains or wailing down corridors either.' Ruth was quite miffed.

'Sorry.' Alice didn't know what else to say. Her head was addled and she wanted to go back to her friends. 'Tell you what, meet me in my cubicle later, after lights out and we can talk more then. Is that ok?'

Ruth pouted, and looked like she was about to protest when two seniors walked into the washroom. Alice busied herself with drying her hands and mumbled a greeting; the two girls acknowledged her but did not stop. Alice followed them with her eyes as they exited through the door Alexandra had come through earlier. When Alice looked back, Ruth was gone.

CHAPTER 13

Questions about Ruth

The students' banter and squeals of reunion became a familiar sound throughout the day. The old girls quickly unpacked or abandoned cases and bags for summer gossip, grouping together in their familiar cliques and circles. It soon became obvious to Alice who hung with whom and who stood out by their popularity, or not as the case may be.

The First Years generally stuck together, unlike the other years, who happily mingled together. As new girls, and the bottom of the rung, they were either ignored, acknowledged politely or teased by mocking Second and Third Years. Alice had little to no contact with the seniors, except those that recognised her and called out 'Just Billy' before disappearing to the depths of the senior dorm, with their coffee and air of superiority. She was beginning to feel the insignificance of being a First Year when she suddenly recognised some familiar faces walking down the Big Dorm corridor.

Mary-Jane, Felicity and Ting were giggling away with each other. Alice felt a surge of camaraderie at seeing the girls she had met earlier in the year and bounded up to them.

'Hi, guys, how's it going?'

The three girls stopped, taken aback by a First Year grinning enthusiastically in front of them. Felicity greeted Alice with a quiet 'Hi Alice' and Ting smiled at her when Mary-Jane declared, 'Ladies, remember your place, we are Third Years now. No time for First Years.' And, cocking her head, she dismissed Alice, dragging her buddies with her. Alice turned to find Bessie and Gale gaping out the curtain at her. Feeling dejected, Alice solemnly made her way back to her cubicle.

The rest of the day had been a mix of meeting other girls, the new routine of meals, assembly and free time for walks, and getting familiar with the general school layout. It was close to lights out and Miss Ash had already announced bedtime. Alice lay in her bed waiting. Her mind raced back through the day's events, weighing up her excitement of being away from home with the longing she now had for her own bed and familiar noises of her home. Thinking of Pete and wondering if he made it back to the hideout or how he was getting on back at school. She'd write to him soon and tell him everything that had happened. Well, almost everything.

Alone with her thoughts, Alice wondered more about Ruth, and what her story was. She could hear the pitter-patter of feet sneaking around the corridor, rushed final conversations and beds creaking as girls settled down for the night. There was the last of the teeth brushing, and then the odd cough. It wasn't long before there was little to be heard other than the deep snoring of a girl off in the far corner of the dorm and the odd mumble as another talked in her sleep. Alice fought to stay awake, her eyelids growing heavier and heavier. Quietness descended on the Big Dorm and Alice drifted off to sleep, eventually giving up on a visit from Ruth.

CHAPTER 14

Settling In

The first few days went by quickly. They had spent most of the time preparing for the school year, getting assigned a classroom, timetables, and books. It had all been very exciting and yet simple at the same time. There really hadn't been any classes as such – more an introduction to their teachers and subjects.

As Kylemore was a 'convent school' Alice had expected the school side of things to be run and taught by nuns. So she was both surprised and relieved to discover that only two of the first-year teachers were nuns.

Sister Ursula taught civics. Alice wasn't really sure what that subject entailed. The tiny little nun spent most of her time recounting stories of the past and what it had been like for her as a student during her own time at Kylemore. She was very sweet, with large eyes that disappeared every time she smiled behind her bottle-end glasses. And she did that a lot. Alice wondered how she could see at all.

And then there was Sister Cecilia. She taught them French and music. Or rather sang it. The girls giggled at first when she glided into the classroom and grabbed the door, swinging it on its hinges, back and forth, calling out, 'Bonjour Mademoiselles, bonjour mes petites, ouvrez la fenêtre s'il vous plaits – Good morning ladies, open the windows please, let the fresh air in', and went off on a chant of French, singing the words as she fanned the room with the classroom door.

Alice liked to listen to her. She thought French sounded beautiful but still didn't understand much by the end of the class besides saying hello and introducing herself. Bessie had teased her, wondering how 'Just Billy' would translate.

Some other nuns taught the seniors, including Dame Mary who taught accounting, and there was a young Italian nun, Sister Catherine, who taught art.

The rest of the teachers were lay teachers, or 'human' as Bessie liked to describe them – although Alice wasn't too sure by the end of the week. There was Mrs Stern who taught history; she nearly re-enacted the battles as she described them, she was so enthusiastic about the past. And there was Miss Byrne, who taught English and physical education. She always wore a tracksuit coming from one to the other, and never stopped moving. 'No wonder she is so skinny,' Bessie had said, relishing another biscuit. 'I'd say she can't eat enough to keep up with the calories she burns. She must be always starving.'

Gale was disappointed to learn that there were only two male teachers: Mr. Toner, who taught them maths, and Mr O'Dea, who taught science. 'They're not much to look at,' Gale moaned one afternoon in Alice's cubicle. 'And what is it with Mr. Toner always twirling at his moustache? The way it curls up at the sides, he's like something out of a British royal painting.'

'I think he is nice,' Bessie said shyly. She bit the quick of her nails.

'You think everyone is nice.' Gale flicked her hair, settling it loosely down her back.

'I think Mr O'Dea is funny,' Alice said, watching Gale as she finger-combed the knots out of her hair.

'Is that funny-weird or funny-ha ha?' Gale asked. 'Probably a bit of both.' Alice thought of Mr O'Dea, his tall skinny frame with dicky-bow, giving them the tour of the laboratory and introducing them to the periodic table while he rocked back and forth on his heels.

'What about Dom Paul?' Gale smiled, adding sarcastically, 'He's a bit of a looker isn't he?'

Both Alice and Bessie grunted. 'He's hardly human,' Alice joked. She pictured the short monk who was the Abbey chaplin. With his snuff and red handkerchiefs, and tidy stature, he walked with a step and an air that was larger than life. Alice always felt nervous around him.

'Ava says he directs the school plays and sometimes does special religion classes,' Bessie said as she examined her finger nails. 'The seniors get to rehearse at his cottage and are served *real* afternoon tea with cakes and little sandwiches and clotted cream.' Bessie paused to think about that, then added, 'She says that while he comes across as all pompous and haughty he can be very nice.' Bessie paused again, 'especially if you are smart and can remember all your lines.'

'Well, that will rule me out then for sure,' Alice said ' I can hardly remember my prayers, never mind any lines for a play. Bet you'll be in his good books though.' Alice nudged Gale. She looked puzzled. 'With acting running in the family, maybe some of your mother's famous genes rubbed off on you.' Gale moaned, nudging Alice back, and went back to examining her hair for split ends.

It was while getting their uniforms that Alice really began to feel as if they were blending in. Alice enjoyed the whole ceremony of it. Any new students, including First Years, lost a good morning of classes as a result of the queuing and measuring for their new clothes.

Sister Ursula was in charge of them and was very particular and proud of how each girl looked wearing the school colours. It had been fairly painless for most – that is until she had to measure some of the larger girls. Bessie had been lucky. Originally she had been panicking about finding a skirt that would fit her, but quickly forgot all about it when, at the last minute, Dame Mary brought in a late arrival. She was introduced as Ana Bamway, and Alice had never seen anyone like her in her life. Judging by the look on Bessie's face, Alice figured she hadn't either. 'Close your mouth Bessie,' Alice had to whisper. 'You'll catch flies if you leave it hanging open like that.'

Ana Bamway was broad as she was tall, with beautiful dark braids twisted in a giant knot trailing half way down her back. There were beaded ends that clicked and clacked, swaying as she made an entrance. Her skin was as black as night and as smooth and shiny as freshly frozen ice on a still, deep pond. Alice smiled shyly at the girl when she looked at her, and was delighted at the wide white smile Ana gave back. As a senior who might miss some crucial classes, Ana was ushered to the front of the queue, and Sister Ursula went into overdrive in measuring and fitting her out.

'I think we will have to order you a blazer, Ana. I don't think I have any suitable in stock,' Sister Ursula said, adding, 'at the moment'.

'That will be just fine, Sister,' Ana beamed at Sister Ursula. 'I don't mind waiting, and if it's not needed, then I don't mind not having it at all.' Sister Ursula smiled and chatted politely with the girl as she fussed back and forth with the measuring tape. The nun looked especially tiny as she circled busily around Ana's buxomly frame.

Alice loved the long friendly lilt of Ana's accent. Images of foreign lands and exotic worlds flashed into her head. She couldn't begin to place where Ana came from, but there was a friendly confidence about her accent that was pleasant to the ear. Alice guessed that Sister Ursula liked it too, as she beamed and nodded at Ana.

Alice also proved a challenge to Sister Ursula, but not for the same reasons as Ana Bamway. 'You really are tiny, aren't you, Alice, and that is saying a lot coming from me,' the nun tittered. 'I don't think the new skirts will fit you. We will have to revert to the old tunics for you. I think I have some of the smaller sizes to spare.' Sister Ursula had explained that the school was phasing out the tunics and bringing in a more modern skirt. Everything else was pretty much the same: plaid blue and white chequered shirt, navy with blue stripe detail on the jumper and the blue blazer with school crest, 'Pax Et Nos Avi', on the chest pocket.

Alice was secretly pleased that the skirts didn't fit. It meant that she would have to wear the same style as some of the seniors. Carrie La Bouche and some of the older girls still wore the grey old-style pinafore, and it seemed a case of the sloppier the better. It wasn't a surprise that the school was phasing them out. There was even a similarity to the uniform that Ruth wore, although hers was the genuine fashion of the twenties. As long as she didn't get any slagging for wearing it, Alice was quite accepting of the two pinafores assigned to her.

★★★

Alice was getting to like the weekends. Friday meant no study period. Girls were free to spend the afternoon as they wished. There was Assembly after supper when Dame Mary would meet them all in the grand Music Room when there would be some announcements, reminders of rules and general notices that the Dame wished to bring to the girls' attention.

Choir practice and Benediction followed. It was a whole new thing for Alice, who followed the train of girls up to the little chapel that was once the castle ballroom for Benediction, which was the Evening Compline, or final evening prayers, for the nuns. On a Friday, the students would join them to recite a litany of prayers and chants. The First Years found it hard to follow, mumbling the replies, darting looks and smiles at each other. Alice found the chant repetitive and surprisingly quiet and relaxing. She found herself making an effort to sing along with the prayer books, but struggled to follow the alien Latin.

Despite Friday evenings being free, some of the really studious girls in exam years had already started to spend their time studying, but most girls just hung out or went for leisurely walks. The evenings were still bright enough, and some of the girls made the most of what light was left.

Bessie and Gale wanted to go for a walk towards the old overgrown walled gardens, but Alice wanted a bit of time for herself and made up an excuse of having to write home or wanting to clean her cubicle.

Alice had spent some time changing her bed linen and towels, dusting and giving her floor a good sweep and mop. Feeling very comfortable now after a shower, and alone in her fresh little space, she happily threw off her shoes and lay on her clean bed with her writing paper and envelopes. She was looking for stickers that she had kept to decorate her letters and was rummaging through her box of notepaper when she got the feeling someone was looking at her.

Alice glanced up to find Ruth sitting on the edge of her bed. 'Where have *you* been?' Alice asked, pleased to see her.

'What do you mean?' Ruth asked confused.

'It's been ages. I was beginning to think I had gone mad and made you up.'

'Really? Gosh, sorry. Sometimes time escapes me. I don't really have much of a concept of it, besides the nights getting longer or a change in the seasons. It has been a while since I have had to keep track of days. Seems like only a moment ago and we were in the washroom.'

Alice thought about that. She supposed it made sense. What was time after all to a ghost when all you had was time?

'What are you doing?' Ruth looked down at Alice's notelet and pen.

'Writing to a friend.'

'How lovely. I used to do that. I loved to write, and of course it was wonderful to get letters from home. We would sometimes get mail twice in the same day. Who are you writing to?'

'My buddy Pete.'

'Your what?'

Alice laughed, 'My friend Peter, I call him Pete for short.'

'Oh. He's a boy. Is he a boyfriend?' Ruth giggled.

'No! Alice declared. 'Pete is just a friend.'

'Who is a boy.'

'Yes, but it is okay nowadays to have a friend who happens to be a boy, you know. It doesn't mean that I am going out with him or anything gross like that.' Alice pictured Peter as she last saw him, with his floppy hair overhanging his forehead and his spray of freckles. Hands shoved into the pockets of his worn corduroy trousers, kicking at stones with his scuffed Adidas trainers. Alice smiled and then grimaced at the thought of herself and Pete being boyfriend and girlfriend.

'Gross?'

Alice sighed. 'Gross, you know, like disgusting or rotten.'

'Seems a bit improper, if you ask me.' Ruth scrunched up her nose.

'Well, he's not. I mean we're not, I mean, there's nothing *improper* about it. It's just, well, he's just Pete.'

Ruth sat by Alice, peering over her shoulder to see what she was writing.

'Do you mind? Letters *are* private.' Alice shut her notelet.

'Sorry.' Ruth looked dejected

'I haven't mentioned anything about you in case you are worried,' Alice added.

'Would he believe you?' Ruth asked animatedly.

'No, probably not. Well I dunno really, maybe. His granny Sally is a bit weird that way. At least I used to think she was. He would often find her talking to herself. She would say she was just chatting to Joe, her late husband. Pete says she's crazy, but I think he wants to believe it. He misses his granddad a lot.'

Alice suddenly felt a longing for home. She shifted on her bed trying to dislodge the heaviness sitting in her stomach. Despite feeling sad and lonely, she wanted to be alone.

'I'm sorry, Ruth, it's been a full-on week and I'm not feeling great. Could you come back later?'

'Alice, I have spent many years waiting to be able to contact someone and you are all I have. You just said you were wondering where I had got to. Can't we talk for a while?'

Alice felt guilty; she couldn't begin to guess how lonely it must be for Ruth. Alice was here less than a month, and while she was really enjoying herself for the most part, there were times when she really missed home. Like now.

'Sorry, of course, make yourself comfortable. Bessie and Gale are gone out for a walk with, it would appear, the rest of the school. Stay a while.' Alice took out a pillow and placed it against the wall of her cubicle for Ruth. Not that she would need it. The two sat there for a moment in silence, and then Alice shifted uncomfortably.

'There *has* been something I would love to ask you,' Alice whispered.

Ruth looked down at her knees, playing with the ghostly hem of her own tunic. 'I suppose you want to know how I died?'

'If you don't mind?' Alice smiled gently at Ruth.

77

'That's the odd thing. I don't remember much. It is all a bit of a blur. I remember being sick and having this sense of great loneliness. Not just from missing my family. No, it is more a sense of being alone. And being afraid.' Ruth's expression saddened as she spoke. 'There are some faces that are familiar to me, but I am not sure who they are. One is a nun. I think she was kind, but she was frightened about something. And there was a man. I think he might have been a friend, but I'm not sure. He wasn't family, but my memory of him is warm and comfortable. And I miss someone dreadfully. Like there is an emptiness I cannot explain, and yet I cannot see their face. It is frustrating because I cannot recall any of the important detail.'

Alice listened carefully, not wanting to interrupt, although it did not make much sense to her.

'I have never had to try and tell someone before, so it is like trying to pull the memories up from a muddy pool. I am sorry, Alice, it is all a bit confusing.'

Alice thought it was, but didn't say. 'Take your time.' She leaned in, curious for more.

'You see, I didn't just become a ghost overnight. I am sure you probably think I died and then puff, there I am, a ghost.' Ruth paused. Alice nodded.

'No, it was really strange. I knew I wasn't in my own body, that is for sure, but I wasn't anywhere else either. I wasn't anywhere real. I must have floated around for a while, because I was conscious of *being,* and then time would go by and I might not *be* for ages.' Alice was scratching her head now, completely puzzled by what Ruth was saying.

'The simplest way to describe it is like dust. For a while I was like a floating dust cloud, aware of my surroundings, but not being in any control of them. Then as time went by I could sort of muster myself together and found that I could move from one place to the next. I had no strength at all in the beginning, and even now I do not have much. That is why it was such an effort to hold the drawer closed on Alexandra.' Alice nodded.

Ruth hung her head low and whispered, 'I found it hard to move away from the classroom, you know, the tower?' Alice nodded again, remembering her first encounter with Ruth. 'And then I would find myself at the cemetery. It was quite a shock to see my own tombstone. Up until then I hadn't really given much thought to my family and home, but the tombstone suddenly made me realise that there was no going back, that it wasn't a bad dream, and that I was really dead.'

'Gosh,' was all that Alice could say. 'So you didn't get killed by a hockey ball.'

'What?'

'Or throw yourself off the bell tower in the Gothic?'

Ruth started to laugh.

'Or get drowned in the lake?' Alice giggled.

'Where did you hear . . .?' Ruth was interrupted by an excited Alice.

'That is what the First Years have been told by the seniors whenever we ask about you.'

'Others have been asking about me? How nice.' Ruth sounded genuinely pleased. 'No, I can honestly say it was none of those. I know I was sick. My parents never came. At least that much is certain.' Ruth went silent.

Alice sighed. She had so many questions to ask, but looking at Ruth and the sadness that hung in her face, she merely said, 'Ruth, for what it is worth, I am very sorry for your trouble.' Alice was about to reach out to comfort Ruth, when suddenly the curtain of her cubicle was yanked open. It was Bessie, panting and very excited.

'Alice, you will never believe it, we were at the mountain

Pokey and . . . ' Bessie had to take in a deep breath, 'they're planning a raid on the Ref TONIGHT!'

And with one leap, Bessie made a dive for the space where Ruth was sitting.

CHAPTER 15

Raiding the Ref

'What do you mean, the Pokey?' Alice glanced about her cubicle; there was no sign of Ruth, and Bessie now filled the space where Ruth had been a moment earlier.

'Yeah, the Pokey, you know, where the seniors go outside for a sneaky fag.' Bessie rolled her eyes at Alice's ignorance. 'There are lots around the estate. The mountain one is closest, there is the boathouse one and the lake one and ... oh, never mind. Anyway, Mary-Jane and some of the Second and Third Years are planning to go down tonight.'

'Go down?' Alice hadn't quite caught up with Bessie's banter.

'Oh Alice, you're not listening.' Bessie was exasperated. 'Down to the Ref, to raid it, get some goodies.'

'But we're hardly here a month.' While it did sound very exciting to Alice, it didn't make a whole lot of sense. Most girls had some of their stash of tuck from home and were not in need of any extra treats just yet.

Tuck was the food stash and survival kit for any boarder. First Years didn't find out about it until too late, as a tuck bag was not exactly something that would be listed on the official 'things to bring to school' list. But meals never seemed to be enough for the growing girls, and there was always a demand for extra treats, chocolate or snacks. There was the tuck shop, which was a small cupboard-like shop that only opened twice a week for an hour to supply all the current sweet favourites of the girls: Wispas, Mars Bars, Marathons, Highland toffee and crisps, and penny sweet treats like Black Jacks, Refreshers, Fizzy Colas, Chocolate Cups, lollipops, and

White Mice. It was run by the Fourth Years as a small business project and they took great pleasure in the control and benefits associated with it.

The post office occasionally had the odd box of Crunchy or Dairy Milk bars, but, for the most part, the girls relied on their own supply of food to boost their sugar calorie count for the day. Hence tuck bags – or suitcases, as was sometimes the case. The American girls always had a great choice of treats, the US being the treats capital of the world. For the first time Alice got to see what a Hershey Chocolate Kiss and Twinkies looked like and to savour the sweet and sour creamed crisps, Pringles. And, boy, did the Americans know how to do big; she had never seen the likes of the tubs of peanut butter and spicy peppers that Tanya had.

Tuck bags came bursting at the seams at the beginning of term and slowly reduced over time, depending on the generosity or greed of a girl. And then there were the enterprising girls who would hoard their stash until others were running out and on a long winter evening make a tidy profit on a bar of chocolate, some even going to the extreme of charging per square. There was always money to be made from the girls who just couldn't wait till daylight hours for the tuck shop or post office.

That was where raiding the Ref came in for the hungry and adventurous who liked the combination of the rush from the raid and the reward of the stash. Organised and controlled by the seniors, it was a big secret mission that consequentially everyone knew about.

'Why go down now?' Alice asked.

'Duh!' Bessie pulled a moronic face. 'Cos they can. Seriously though, Mary-Jane says that they watch out for special deliveries and there was a HB van outside today.'

'HB? As in ice cream?' Alice felt saliva fill her cheeks.

'Yes. And maybe even some yoghurt.' Bessie licked her lips at the thought. 'Whatever about the yoghurt though, I really would love some raspberry ripple ice cream.'

'But you're, I mean, we're not going, are we?' Alice asked. Bessie's excitement was contagious. Alice both loved and feared the idea at the same time.

'Nah, apparently you have to be *invited* to go, and we are *too new* yet.' Bessie punctuated the 'invited' and 'too new' with her fingers for emphasis.

'Oh.' Alice was disappointed, now that they were being excluded.

At that moment, Gale casually strolled into the cubicle and sat on the stool at the head of Alice's bed.

'So what do you think, Gale?' Bessie jumped up onto her knees on the bed.

'About what?' Gale started to examine the end of her long plait for split ends. Someone had turned on their ghetto-blaster in the background. Gale started singing along with The Eurythmics' song, *Sweet Dreams*.

'How can you not be excited?' Bessie squirmed. 'Raiding the Ref!'

Gale stopped singing and swung her plait back over her shoulder. 'Ah, that's easy. Because *we're* not the ones going.'

Alice smiled at Gale. 'So how do they do it? Doesn't it mean having to go through the nuns' Enclosure?'

During the day, the girls would gain access to the Ref for meals by one central big staircase located behind a secure solid door near Dame Mary's office. It was a purpose-built staircase that linked an old castle corridor on the first floor with what was the castle's library, now Ref, on the ground floor. This door was locked and inaccessible outside meal times. However, there was a whole network of rooms and passages that snaked behind the public and school area known as the

Enclosure. This was the private area of the nuns. Various doors and entrances pocketed the building for the nuns to come and go to their own enclosed area from the school. Students were not allowed or welcome.

Alice felt guilty at the mere thought of it. How thrilling.

Bessie explained what she knew about it. 'I know you'd think I'd have an in with Ava and what actually goes on, but she doesn't tell me anything.' Bessie paused, 'Well, not a whole lot anyway.'

Alice shifted in closer to hear the detail.

'The Knight Raiders control everything.'

'The Knight Raiders?' Alice sniggered. 'Is that knight with a K or an N?'

'K', Bessie answered.

'Sounds like a bad movie,' Gale offered.

'Yeah, I know.' Bessie nodded. 'Anyway they are mostly Third Years, with some chosen few from other years. Of course, the seniors know when the raid goes down and take their own cut, but they rarely actually go down themselves, the novelty's worn off for them. Ava says why go yourself if you can have some minions do it for you and still benefit from the food treasure?' Bessie sat back, delighted with the attention.

Alice found herself warming to the idea. 'How cool! So how do we get to be invited?'

'That's where we luck out, my friend.' Gale had started to examine her nails. 'While the idea did appeal to me too, it would seem that even if we are invited to raid the Ref, we have to pass some test first. You know, prove that we are up for it.'

'Oh?' Alice was even more interested.

'Yeah!' Bessie jumped in ahead of Gale. 'Ava said it involves the Gothic and retrieving some trophy. I tried to push her for more information, but she wouldn't tell me.'

'Not just "some trophy".' Gale glanced skyward impatiently and then looked directly at Alice. 'THE Trophy.'

Alice was laughing. 'You're kidding. Surely sneaking into the Gothic would be more troublesome than going into the Enclosure?'

'Nope.' Bessie smiled back at Alice. 'The Gothic was dee, de-con, oh you know, made un-holy.'

'Deconsecrated,' Gale offered. She reached for a nail file on Alice's dresser.

'Whatever,' Bessie hurried. 'Anyway, the Enclosure is sacred. Mary-Jane was *very* serious when she was telling us.'

Gale frowned for emphasis. 'Apparently you have to sneak out of school, go down to the Gothic at night, find a way in and retrieve the hidden Trophy and bring it back to Mary-Jane. They go through this initiation every year with aspiring Knight Raiders. Mary-Jane is kinda leading it this year. Every year they replace the Trophy for the next sucker. Of course Mary-Jane didn't quite say it like that, she made the whole thing very dramatic and mysterious.'

'You should have seen it. The whole Pokey went silent,' Bessie whispered. 'Everyone hanging on every word she said.'

'What were ye guys doing in the Pokey?' Alice was sorry she hadn't gone for the walk now.

'Oh, I went to ask Ava if she had taken my new fingerless gloves, mine are missing, she's always taking my things, thought she might have them, but she didn't,' Bessie pouted.

'I didn't know Ava smoked?' Alice asked, dismissing the missing fingerless gloves.

'Oh, she doesn't, but she likes to hang out there with the rest of the seniors. It's really cool up there.'

'So what do you think the Trophy is? A chalice?' Gale interrupted as she continued to file her nails.

85

'Sounds a bit dodgy to me, like an opportunity for the third years to make fools of some First Years,' Alice said.

'You may think so, but if you want to become a Knight Raider, you have to retrieve the Trophy.' Bessie was wagging her finger jokingly at Alice.

'Okay, but surely breaking out to get to the Gothic would be more difficult than sneaking down into the Ref?' Alice still couldn't quite make sense of the logic.

'Yeah, I thought so too, especially as it involves getting out of school after lights out and the back gates are locked, but Mary-Jane said that side of it is sorted, whatever that is supposed to mean.' Bessie shrugged. 'Anyway, if we want to get into the Ref, you have to meet the Gothic challenge first. And that challenge is not up for anyone. One First Year is picked. There are *certain criteria* that have to be met. For that we talk to Mary-Jane.' Gale stood up and stretched, then put her hands in her skirt pockets. It was obvious that she didn't want to listen anymore.

Bessie stood too. 'All this talk of the Ref is making me hungry. Is it time for supper yet?'

Alice checked her watch and nodded. 'Hmm, I can't help think that there is more here than they are saying, but no harm in finding out is there? Let's go for a walk tomorrow after breakfast and take another look at the Gothic.'

'Good idea,' Bessie beamed. 'Can we go now? My stomach is stuck to my back I'm so hungry?'

'Yes, Bessie,' both Alice and Gale sung in unison.

CHAPTER 16

Initiation

'A bottle of wine?' Alice asked incredulously. 'The Trophy is a bottle of old altar wine?'

To Alice it sounded like one big joke and that someone was pulling her leg.

Mary-Jane just stared at her, expressionless.

'It's not just *any* bottle of altar wine. Of course, any *real* bottles of altar wine would have been removed years ago by Dom Paul or whoever, but *this* bottle of wine has been passed down through the years by preceding Knight Raiders and is symbolic of a great line of students that have *successfully* retrieved and then returned it to the Gothic, unnoticed, unobserved and undiscovered.' Mary-Jane paused for effect. 'It is not about the bottle of wine, but what *you* can prove to us in fulfilling the mission. It is a test of courage and fidelity, a rite of passage. Not anyone is invited to try out for it, Alice, and if you are not prepared to take it seriously then you can forget getting anywhere near the Ref.'

'No, of course, Mary-Jane. I mean, when you put it like that . . . I am honoured.' Alice fidgeted on the spot and then added, 'I'm game.'

The small group of girls had silently met at the door to the back stairs. Ting and Felicity stood behind Mary-Jane, like two bodyguards, arms folded, doing their best to look very serious and official. Alice was feeling quite nervous, and any previous bravado was now replaced with apprehension about the task ahead. She wished Bessie and Gale could be there now, but was equally delighted to have been the chosen one. Alice wasn't sure why she had been selected, and there was some hinting by Mary-Jane about Alice having to prove she was as much as a tomboy as she made herself out to be, but Alice wasn't going to ask too much about that now. Bessie and Gale were disappointed, of course, and a bit miffed that Alice had been chosen over them – Bessie thinking that, because she had Ava for a sister, she might have been chosen, and Gale for her own reasons. But the excitement of Alice having to go soon took over any ill feeling, and there was great anticipation that Saturday night as Bessie and Gale waited.

Breaking into the Gothic church to steal a bottle of altar wine seemed quite doable in daylight hours, but Alice was now having second thoughts in the quiet dark of night.

Alice felt strange standing now in the corridor that usually buzzed with the traffic of girls in between classes or study, and which now harboured hidden shadows and a hushed history. Alice pulled her coat about her and stood still, mentally checking off her list of what had to be accomplished. Secretly she wished that Ruth might appear. Alice would take her company if she couldn't have that of Bessie or Gale. But as Ruth's timing was a bit erratic and unpredictable, she couldn't always be relied on to show up when Alice actually wanted her.

'So you know what you have to do?' Mary-Jane asked authoritatively.

'Yes Mary-Jane.' Alice listed off what she had been asked to remember. 'Sneak, Enter, Retrieve.' Alice paused, trying to recall what came next in the list of actions. Her mind drew a blank. Mary-Jane looked expectantly at her. Then Alice remembered. 'Evade, Resist, Survive, Escape!' Alice sighed with relief.

'No bottle of wine, no Knight Raiders,' Mary-Jane summarised officially.

Alice nodded.

'Be as quick as you can, and do not get caught, or you will have hell to pay.' Mary-Jane opened the back door slowly. 'Take this to open the back gate, and return it directly to me or suffer the consequences. No questions asked.' She shoved a large brass key into Alice's hand and pushed her out the door.

A draft of cold air blew up the back stairs and wafted round Alice's legs, carrying smells of the dark night and damp back yard. She pulled her hat on tight below her ears. Using the electric light of the yard below to find her way down the stairs to the back gate, Alice stepped forward gingerly. The yard gate was locked nightly to keep the girls in and strangers out. Alice inserted the key that Mary-Jane gave her and was surprised how easily it turned. Glancing around her, she crept out and quietly closed and locked the gate behind her again.

It was as if she had stepped into a scene from some old horror movie, as the moonlight reflected off the granite of the castle and the charcoal black of the forest drew in around her. After taking a deep breath for confidence, the air tasting of damp wood and leaves, Alice crept around the side of the castle, paused a moment and then quickly made her way down the path towards the Gothic, glancing occasionally behind her. The odd light here and there in the nuns' quarters hinted at some life there, but otherwise Alice was alone with the night.

The canopy of birch and oak trees offered little reassurance as she made her way swiftly towards the Gothic, fighting the fear of someone following her. She took some comfort in the melody of the cascading brook that fed the lake nearby and imagined the path before her in daylight instead of the dark of night. The moon offered some light, and Alice was grateful for its company and serenity.

The Gothic church loomed ahead, eerily silhouetted

against the night sky and backdrop of the mountain. Quickly making her way to the door of the miniature cathedral, her eyes followed the line of the limestone exterior and focused for a while on the projecting buttresses and carved gargoyles. They appeared to sneer down upon her now, mocking her efforts. Alice made her way up the few steps to the entrance and gave the double doors a shove. As anticipated, the loose chain gave way and the doors opened a slither. Bitter, stale air wafted out as she peered in the narrow gap.

Sizing up the small gap in the chain, Alice realised why she had been chosen. It wasn't that she was special or liked by the seniors. It was simply because she was small and neat enough to get in. She was about to remove her coat when a movement down the path caught her eye. She held her breath and felt fear creep up inside her. Her eyes were drawn upwards. A wind slowly moved through the trees. Alice watched as the tree tops swayed, one after another, each tipping the other with a slow movement stirring them into life. Convincing herself that it was just nerves and that the coast was clear, Alice took off her coat and shoved it through the gap ahead of her. Glancing over her shoulder, she turned sideways to the opening, squatted low and slowly bent and twisted herself in through the gap under the chain.

Now that she was inside, Alice felt a little more secure from being caught, although she was still quite nervous. The interior of the church was dark save what moonlight filtered through dust-encrusted windows flanking either side of the chancel. The sour damp and musty air caught her at the back of her throat and sent a chill through her. She was happy to pull on her coat again.

Alice made her way slowly up the centre aisle and took in her surroundings. There was a plain glass tracery window at the altar, and midway on the south side was a beautiful stained-glass window. On closer inspection, Alice could make out five panels, each with a different angel, the titles underneath reading, 'Fortitude, Faith, Charity, Hope and Chastity'. Alice was moved at the image and felt saddened that the church had been as good as abandoned. Surely it would be more beneficial to have the church restored and open to the public. She imagined what it might be like to get married there.

Under the window were initials and names of other girls who had gone before her. Alice was reminded that she was only one of many who must have faced the same challenge and fears as she now did.

Feeling more at ease and focusing on her task Alice slowly made her way up towards the altar in search of the vestry. She had spotted a small doorway leading off the altar to the right when a sudden loud noise and bang made her jump. She stifled her scream. Someone was at the door, and Alice could hear the rattling of the chain. Alice rushed towards her only exit, slamming into a well-jammed and secured double door.

CHAPTER 17

Panic in the Gothic

Alice's first reaction was to panic. She felt nauseous, and a cold and clammy sweat broke out on her skin. Grabbing the doors from the inside, she shook them hard and loud, shouting at the top of her voice. Alice could hear footsteps and laughter on the other side and then she recognized the mocking snort of Alexandra. 'Open the door, Alexandra, I know it's you. Don't be such a cow. Come on, let me out.'

Alice called out in vain. All she could hear was the lonely echo of her own voice lost to the wind and dark outside. She stood for a moment and then gathered her senses about her. The Gothic, after all, had been a public place; surely that meant there was another exit from the building. Making her way back up the aisle and into the vestry, Alice took in the small room with its spiral staircase leading up into the tall square tower. Shuddering at the thought of a murdered nun, Alice decided that the tower would not offer a means of escape. She ventured further into the corner room and checked the miniature arched doorway where there might have been an alternative exit from the chapel. It was locked. Cobwebs and dust proved that it had been a long time since this door had been open.

Glancing frantically around, Alice spotted a small cupboard. There, looking at odds with the place, stood a bottle of wine. The Trophy. She decided she may as well take it. After all if she escaped the Gothic she would need to prove she had completed the challenge. It was a small dusty old bottle of altar wine that no doubt was well past its best-before date. Alice smiled at the idea that this crusty, mottled looking bottle of vinegar was a great symbol of triumph. Picking it up and checking it for leaks, Alice took out a pillowcase from her coat pocket and wrapped up the bottle well before stuffing it in her coat. Feeling the chill, Alice pulled on her coat tighter around herself.

Where was Ruth when she needed her?

Alice stood for a moment wondering if there was a way to summon Ruth to help her get out. Neither of them had figured out a way yet, and days could go by when Ruth would think it was just minutes.

Alexandra was pure trouble, and Alice was furious that she had got caught by her. Then Alice wondered if the locking in was part of the initiation, that Mary-Jane's lot might be testing her even further. Alice hoped that Alexandra hadn't gone out of her way to interfere with the initiation. She had taken a serious dislike to Alice, and this would be the perfect opportunity to set Alice up for the worst.

Alice walked back into the chancel and scanned the walls for any broken windows or missed exits. She had a creeping realisation that she would not get out of this easily and she did not like the prospect of being found much later into the hours of tomorrow, never mind the idea of having to spend the night imprisoned within the Gothic walls. She would be missed at the Abbey, and Alice did not relish the action Dame Mary would take.

Expulsion was the punishment for any girl caught outside of the Abbey after lock-down. And the shame of that was worse than any fear she had been feeling. A sense of panic was quickly flooding her mind. All sounds became exaggerated in Alice's head, the interior of the Gothic being a vacuum compared to all the scratching and wailings of nature outside. The stillness of the church pressed in on her, and Alice imagined the walls moving in closer.

A noise from near the altar startled Alice. Glancing furtively out the vestry opening, she was relieved to see that it was Ruth.

'So my senses were right.' Ruth smiled at Alice. 'I had a strange feeling that you needed some help.'

'You can say that again,' Alice sighed with relief. 'Alexandra, she's locked me in.'

'That Alexandra is a real mischief maker. She really has something in for you.'

Alice sat down slowly, first pulling the seat of her coat well under her for warmth against the cold marble altar step, careful of the bottle in the pocket.

'I mean, she is rather stupid to think that this would only get *me* in trouble,' Alice cribbed. 'After all, if I was to get caught here, there would be all sorts of questions as to how I even got out beyond the school backyard, whatever about getting through there.' Alice pointed at the double doors. 'I might not be the only one to be expelled, and she would have to live with the Knight Raiders' wrath!'

'I'm not so sure.' Ruth sat next to Alice. 'Alexandra can be crafty when she is being cruel. But I wouldn't worry anymore now.' Ruth stood up suddenly. 'Because, my dear friend, I have an escape route for you.'

'Need I remind you that I cannot walk through walls?' Alice raised her eyebrows.

Ruth fluttered her hand dismissively at Alice. 'No, this is definitely humanly possible, although it may involve a bit of gymnastics on your part.'

Alice's curiosity was tweaked, and she felt a warm rush of excitement replace her previous foreboding. Ruth had moved off to the side and stood grinning at Alice.

'What are you smiling about?'

Ruth pointed to the floor where there was the outline of

a square that Alice had previously missed. Alice stared at it for a moment and then the penny dropped.

'Oh my God, it's a trapdoor!' Alice squatted down on the panelling and tried to prize her fingers in along where the edge was now caked with years of dust and neglect.

'It was designed so that coffins could be lowered to the vaults below,' Ruth explained. 'The first were the remains of three of the nuns who had fled Ypres, but I think it must have proved too difficult for the nuns after that and they created the cemetery outside.'

'Ugh. You're saying it is a tomb down there? I don't like the sound of that,'

'Well, it is your only option for getting out of here to-night, Alice.'

Alice begrudgingly squatted down by the trapdoor and tried to open it.

'Crikey, they must have had a lot of fun trying to get the coffins down there.' Alice shook the pinched feeling from her fingers. She took in her surroundings, hoping to find something that could wedge the trap door open, but to no avail, and then remembered the brass key in her pocket. She used it to scrape clear the dirt from the rim of the trapdoor and then attempted another pull. 'Can you help? It's still a bit stuck.'

Ruth mustered up what strength she could. Bending, she followed close to where Alice was gripping the floorboards, and on the count of three the two girls pulled. There was some slight resistance, and then the trapdoor gave way with a sucking sound, revealing a dark, sour-smelling abyss.

CHAPTER 18

Into the Abyss

A lice peered in. 'I can't see a thing down there, how far down is it?'

'Not too far, but enough that you won't be able to drop down, best to hang and perhaps get a footing on one of the empty catacombs below.'

'Cat-a-what?' Alice didn't like the sound of that.

'They are the tombs that were never used. They're set up like big shelves from the floor towards the ceiling.'

'Eugh, that just sounds totally creepy.' Alice shivered.

'Take my word for it, other than lots of cobwebs, a few stalactites, and some muddy ground, there isn't anything else down there.' Ruth looked Alice straight in the face.

'I take it you didn't have much luck with making any contact with the nuns buried there,' Alice said as she sat on the edge of the trap door, her feet dangling over the edge.

'I gave up on them a long time ago. No, I am pretty much on my own round here, despite all the potentials from the cemetery. I used to think that each new burial might bring some sort of company, but they all just bypassed my world without so much as a how-do-you-do.'

Alice felt sorry for Ruth, how lonely it must be, and frustrating. All those years, and others dying and passing on, and she stuck waiting. Alice often wondered if it was something that Ruth controlled herself, to leave this world for the next. But then Alice could only guess at what the options must be. All she knew was what she had read about in books, stories based on myths and legends. It would seem that Ruth herself didn't know anyway, or wasn't letting on. Either way, Alice wasn't much help to her. She thought a change of subject would be a good idea, and an opportunity to stall having to throwing herself into the abyss below.

'So who are the nuns down there anyway?'

'Well, you know how their original Abbey in Ypres was destroyed during the Great War, and the nuns fled to Britain?' Alice nodded. 'Well it didn't happen overnight. They had to take refuge in various houses and never really settled until they acquired Kylemore Castle.'

Ruth sat next to Alice. 'Once the Abbey had been officially established here at Kylemore, it was decided to exhume the remains of the three nuns that had died since leaving Ypres. They had been buried temporarily in Wexford. I think the Lady Abbess at the time thought it was fitting that their final resting place should be here among the rest of the community.'

Ruth started to giggle and then went on to explain. 'There is a story that they didn't move all three at once, and the first, the remains of old Abbess Berge, was transported by van ahead of the others. Apparently there was a bit of a mixup and her coffin was lost en route.'

'What? Alice gasped. 'How could they lose a coffin?'

Ruth bent down peering into the blackness beneath them.

'Oh it was something to do with the time of the Troubles, and that coffins were often used to transport guns. It was thought by the transporter that her coffin might be mistaken by the authorities as one harbouring weapons, and when he came upon a crossroad checkpoint in the distance, he thought it best to hide the coffin in a nearby hayshed. The transporter went off to the local tavern to wait out his time. I'm sure the farmer got a fine fright on finding a coffin in his shed. Fortunately, he had his senses and knew not to alert the local constabulary and headed into the village's tavern instead.

'Well, I suppose you can imagine how it sorted itself out. But it did mean the nuns were at a loss for a day or two as to what happened to poor Abbess Berge. There wasn't half as much excitement for Dame Rossiter and Dame Magner who followed on after her. Still, at least they found peace in the end.'

'Right.' Alice wriggled on the edge of the trapdoor. 'Best to get a move on before Miss Ash misses me. How is it looking down there?'

Ruth disappeared down the hole, and Alice could hear her voice beneath her. 'It is about a twelve foot drop, so if you can slowly lower yourself down and take a foothold on the edge of the top catacomb, I mean, top shelf.'

'Best take this first, if you can?' Alice had taken off her coat with the Trophy intact and lowered it down in the darkness towards Ruth.

'Ok, you can let it drop.' There was a squeak from Ruth followed by a dull thump, and Alice flinched. 'Oops, sorry, didn't quite catch that,' Ruth shouted up to Alice. 'But it's fine, no broken glass!'

'Oh for the love of . . .' Impatient to check, Alice had turned onto her stomach and was lowering her legs, using the strength of her arms to slowly lever herself down into the dark.

'To your right, throw your leg outwards to the right as you lower yourself, the shelf is just there. A bit more, over, over.'

Alice couldn't see a thing, and her grip white-knuckled as she kicked outwards at the empty air beneath her, taking guidance from Ruth until at last she felt something solid beneath her toes.

'Don't forget to pull the trapdoor over again.'

'Crikey, now you tell me.' Alice struggled a bit, but managed to grasp the trapdoor and pull it back in place. She was regretting the situation now, feeling her strength wane. Her arm muscles quivered as she lowered herself slowly, her muscles paining with the effort. Her toes were cramping, and she put every effort into finally tugging the trapdoor back into place. Stretching out with one hand, she grasped the edge of the catacomb and pulled herself into the open tomb.

Her eyes having adjusted to the darkness, Alice could make out Ruth below her. Alice felt she was sitting on top of a very morbid book case, except these shelves were not designed to hold books.

'The next bit is relatively easy,' Ruth teased. 'Just the floor is just a bit muddy, so mind you don't slip when you land. Don't forget to bend your knees.'

'Just like that!' Alice joked. Taking a moment and a quick breath, she let herself drop.

The floor greeted her sooner than expected, but she regained her composure relatively gracefully.

'Ta-dah!' Alice sang out, raising her arms in the air, as if she had just completed a perfect ten gymnastic dismount.

'Gold Medal to Alice Stone,' Ruth beamed at Alice, giving her a round of applause.

Alice shook her arms, dusted herself off and picked up her coat. Happy that the Trophy was safe and intact, she turned to Ruth.

'Okay, from chapel to tomb, what now?'

'Follow me.' Ruth walked further into the vaults.

Alice followed Ruth's voice, conscious of her footing and of something soft and slippery beneath her feet.

'This way, there are small windows over here that lead to the outside.' Ruth guided her across the vault. Alice could see the faint outline of a tiny door flanked by small stone-arched windows. There was no glass. Peering out the small window, Alice could just make out some stone steps leading up from the other side of the door to ground level. The reality of being way below hit home to Alice. She felt a shiver crawl up her spine. She reached for the door handle.

'I'm afraid the door is bolted secure and well locked for decades,' Ruth explained. 'You are going to have to squeeze through the opening of one of the windows.'

'How did we miss that before?' Alice wondered aloud.

'Most girls miss it from the outside,' Ruth explained. 'It is right around the back of the church. As you know, it is well overgrown there. You would have to crawl through the bushes to get anywhere near it. The steps are almost hidden as they go down from ground level. And even if you did find it, the door is well sealed and the stone windows out of reach from the outside. Some have tried over the years, but no one has ever got in that way.' Ruth smiled. 'You are the first to approach the windows from the inside.'

Alice sized up the tiny opening and figured that with some clever twisting and climbing she could manage it. She first pushed her coat through, mindful of its delicate contents, and let it drop gently to the ground outside. It took some leg stretching, and a bit of contortion, but Alice soon found herself on the outer step, looking back up from below ground level. She stopped for a moment.

'Can't rest now, my dear, you still have to get back to the dorm before Miss Ash misses you.' Ruth encouraged the breathless Alice onwards.

'Blimey, I can't believe I got out of that. Thanks again, Ruth. I owe you big time.'

Alice picked up her coat, checking again for the bottle of wine and backdoor key, and started back on the track towards the Abbey.

'Nothing to it, all a familiar haunt to me, if you don't mind the pun.' Ruth smiled at Alice. 'Now that you are okay, I'll go on and see if I can check on Miss Ash's whereabouts. See if the coast is clear back at the Abbey.'

Ruth disappeared before Alice could object. She would have preferred to have some company rather than walk back to the Abbey alone, but Ruth was already gone.

CHAPTER 19

Night Rider

Imagining what the seniors might think of her success, and excited at what Bessie and Gale's reaction would be to her adventure, Alice hurried along, using the light of the moon to guide her. Shadows in the trees danced in the night breeze, branches contorting and scraping in the night air. Dark clouds moved across the sky, and Alice quickened her pace.

She started to brood over Alexandra and how she would take revenge, when a sudden noise made her stop. Beyond the bushes, Alice could hear two muffled agitated voices. Bessie had pointed the area out previously as the boathouse Pokey, and Alice figured that's where the noise was coming from now. Nervous but curious, Alice found herself skirting the ruins of the boathouse. She was surprised to hear the low guttural voice of a boy. She snuck in for a closer look.

'Get off! Stop!' a girl's voice demanded.

'Ah come on, just a quick one.'

Alice crept in closer into the bushes. She could just make out their silhouettes against the light of the moon now glittering on the lake beyond, but she couldn't see for sure who it was. Feeling slightly embarrassed at coming across the two, but knowing that the girl was in trouble, Alice wondered what to do.

Alice had heard rumours about senior girls who would sneak out in the night to link up with boys. But Alice had never known whether or not to believe the rumours. They were known as Night Riders as opposed to the more innocent Knight Raiders. First Years never knew for sure who they were, or how they were getting out, but there was great excitement and many an evening spent gossiping about who it might be.

Alice had to think quickly as now the boy was beginning to get a little more forceful, and she could see that the girl was beginning to struggle. In his turning, the moon cast some light on his face and Alice recognised him as Paddy John, son of PJ, a part-time estate handyman. He sometimes accompanied his dad at the weekend on odd jobs about the Abbey and would often flirt cheekily with the seniors. When he was on site he was never far from his father's side, much to the relief of the girls, and probably that of the nuns.

Hoping to distract them, Alice picked up a large stick and snapped it in two.

The girl pushed Paddy John. 'Paddy stop. Please. Someone is coming!' Paddy John paused for a moment, listening, but then persisted.

Alice decided she needed to do something more and summoned the deepest voice she could, 'What's going on in there?' Then thinking quickly, she scaled the tree beside her, guessing that Paddy John would not think of looking skyward to find where the voice had come from.

Paddy John stopped, then stepped forward to search the thicket under Alice, his eyes peering nervously into the dark. Glancing back at the girl, he mumbled something before escaping along the shore line. The frightened girl scanned the bushes. With the coast clear, Alice climbed down and made her presence known by pushing her way into the clearing 'Are you okay?' The girl turned, and Alice found herself staring at a very surprised and dishevelled looking Tanya.

'Alice, is that you?' Tanya pulled herself together and, somewhat relieved, said, 'My gawd, you scared the life out of me. Where did you come from?'

'The Gothic.' Alice kicked a stone, waiting for Tanya as she tidied herself up and made her way towards Alice, ducking under branches.

'Oh. So you were the *Chosen One?*'

'Humph, yeah.' Alice held back the branches for Tanya. They made it out onto the path and headed back towards the Abbey.

'So how did you get on?' Tanya broke the awkward silence.

'Oh, not bad, I'm here, aren't I.' Alice made a feeble smile. 'And I got the Trophy.'

'Good for you.' Tanya smiled sincerely at Alice.

'No thanks to A Certain Miss Someone,' Alice added and frowned at the thought of the interfering Alexandra.

'What do you mean?'

Alice went into detail, omitting any Ruth bits, about her adventure. She wasn't sure if she should tell about the trapdoor, but so wanting to share her excitement, she revealed the discovery, making out that she found it on her own.

'Wow, that's amazing.' Tanya had stopped walking to take in the full impact of the trapdoor. 'No one has ever mentioned that before, I am sure no one has any idea that it exists. And it leads to the vaults? Fantastic. Alice that is great. How cool!'

Alice couldn't contain the wide grin of pride despite feeling somewhat guilty that it was Ruth who had pointed it out to her.

'Oh, I would love to try that one out. But I think I am gone beyond fitting through the gap. I don't think I would get in with these.' Tanya patted her well-endowed chest. 'These have their disadvantages, you know.'

Embarrassed, Alice looked down at her feet as she walked.

'Alice, I think you should keep the trapdoor a secret for now though, don't you?'

Alice wasn't sure what Tanya was getting at.

'No way!' Alice stopped walking.

'Hang on, hear me out.' Tanya said sympathetically. 'I think Alexandra should be kept in the dark as to how you escaped. After all, she will be expecting the you-know-what to hit the fan later this morning. I think we might enjoy the look on her face to see you come down to breakfast.' Tanya started to walk again, and then added smiling, 'It will kill her to try and figure out how you got out of the Gothic.'

'Not soon enough,' Alice mumbled, a hatred for the girl boiling up inside her.

Keeping an eye on the dark shadow of the castle looming ahead, the girls crept along its walls. Alice made a start for the gate, when she realised that Tanya was veering in another direction up the cliff side.

Whispering low, Alice asked her 'Where are you going? I have the back door key.'

Tanya squatted low and gently called back. 'We can't be seen to come in together. It will just . . . complicate things.' Tanya glanced back up the hill. 'You take the back stairs. I will make my own way in.' At this Tanya nodded towards the mountain.

'Where . . ?' Alice was about to ask, but Tanya just tapped the side of her nose. 'Night Rider's prerogative.' Tanya turned to go, but Alice nervously whispered at her again.

'Tanya, whatever about the trapdoor, what about the . . . rest of tonight?' Alice tried to avoid referring to the rough and tumble with Paddy-John.

'I won't tell if you don't.' Alice could just make out the outline of Tanya's smiling face. 'Deal,' a relieved Alice replied.

'Deal,' Tanya copied. 'Thanks, Alice,' Tanya added more sombrely, and with a quick salute she disappeared up the hillside.

CHAPTER 20

Trophy

Alice was very disappointed not to find someone waiting for her at the top of the back stairs. She fretted briefly, wondering if she should wait or head back up to the Big Dorm, fearing she would get caught by Miss Ash. Deciding that it would be better to be caught upstairs after lights out rather than hovering around the backstairs, she made her way up to the dorm. Only silence and a still darkness greeted her. The dorm was quiet except for the odd grumblings by someone talking in their sleep.

Alice made her way silently to her own cubicle where she quickly undressed and wondered what to do with the Trophy. Waiting to see if Mary-Jane or the others would show, Alice struggled to stay awake in her warm, cosy bed, but it was not long when sleep came. She felt as if she had just closed her eyes when the shrill voice of Miss Ash's morning call pulled her out of a deep, dreamless sleep.

Jumping up out of bed and checking on the Trophy brought the previous night's adventure back. Alice had just finished getting washed and dressed when she heard the approach of running feet followed by a breathless Bessie and Gale.

'My God, you're here. We had almost given up on you.' Bessie lumped herself on Alice's bed.

'Yeah, we had a pretty close call with Ash, she was asking for you at lights out.' Gale followed in behind Bessie.

'What did you say?' Alice did not like the idea of Miss Ash on her back.

'Oh, I told her that you had gotten your period and were

in the toilets,' Gale stated matter-of-factly. Bessie sniggered.

'Eugh! Did you have to?' Alice was grossed out, not by the idea but by Miss Ash knowing anything personal about her.

'Well, it certainly stopped her asking any more about you.'

'Never mind that,' Bessie interrupted. 'Tell us what happened. What took you so long? I was sick to my stomach for you. We were waiting for ages, and then hanging around got too suspicious. Even Mary-Jane and the others had to retreat to their cubicles.'

Alice recounted the night's adventure up to her getting locked in at the Gothic.

'That conniving little cow.' Gale frowned in anger. 'What was she at?'

'Crikey, you must have been terrified. How did you get out?' Bessie's eyes were wide with excitement.

Alice went on to tell about her adventure at the Gothic and decided that she could share finding the trapdoor with her two buddies. She dramatised her descent into the vaults and the squeeze through the windows, without mentioning the help of Ruth or the discovery of Tanya with Paddy John. Alice was quite animated and really getting into the story when Ruth appeared on her dresser.

'Alice?' Gale noticed that Alice had stopped talking and was staring somewhere behind her.

'Huh, what? Oh yeah, sorry.' Alice didn't like the look Ruth had; she was pouting and had her arms crossed, listening to Alice's account of the night's events. On mentioning the Trophy, Alice went to her dresser to retrieve the proof of her night's prowl. She tried to ignore Ruth and went to pull open her top drawer. Ruth held the drawer in place with her leg, sticking her tongue out at Alice. Alice had to give a good tug to get by her.

'Damn drawer's always getting stuck,' Alice mumbled as

she glared at Ruth. Pulling aside her clothes and taking out the pillowcase, she unwrapped the Trophy.

'Is that it?' Bessie took it from Alice's hand. 'All that fuss and bother over this mouldy old bottle!'

Gale glanced out through the curtain, listening to the declining footfalls in the corridor. 'Come on, nearly everyone is gone, we better make a move or we will miss breakfast.'

Alice suddenly realised how hungry she was. All the exertion from the previous night had taken its toll. And she couldn't wait to see Alexandra's face.

'Let's go.' She glanced questioningly at Ruth, mouthing, 'What's wrong with you?' so the others couldn't see her. Ruth turned her head away, ignoring Alice.

'When do you have to hand it over?' Bessie asked as Alice tucked the bottle away in the drawer again.

'I'm not sure. I suppose I have to give it to Mary-Jane.' Alice paused. 'Do you think getting locked in is part of the whole initiation?' Alice asked.

'Hardly,' Gale said. 'If they didn't think there was another means of escape, it wouldn't be in their interest to have someone locked in there overnight. Like, finding the trapdoor would be part of the test. But if they didn't know about the trap door . . ?'

'Bet you they will have a thing or two to say to Alexandra when they find out,' Bessie added.

'No! Not a word to them about her,' Alice jumped in. 'Let's just let it be between her and me, or us as the case is. I want to see her stew in it for a while.'

'I will enjoy seeing Alexandra's face when she sees you at breakfast,' Gale teased.

'Oh my god, you're right.' Bessie was delighted at the thought, and she dragged the other two towards the Ref.

★★★

Alexandra turned a pale grey when she saw Alice descend the stairs into the Ref. She was sitting at her usual table talking with her cronies when Alice strolled confidently past their table, staring at the open-mouthed Alexandra. Bessie could hardly contain herself as she followed behind. Alice didn't look back but did scan the room for Tanya, but to no avail, so looked to see if Mary-Jane and her gang were down for breakfast. Mary-Jane had been watching Alice and when they made eye contact, Alice smiled nervously and nodded. Mary-Jane nodded back, expressionless. It was only when Alice finished her breakfast and was taking her bowl and cup to the slop trolley that Mary-Jane beckoned her over to the senior table.

Gale and Bessie watched as Alice made her way over.

'So, Alice, did you have a successful evening?' Mary Jane sat between Felicity and Ting who looked on with interest. The rest of the table pretended to ignore Alice and continued eating their cereal.

'You could say that.' Alice was feeling confident but still not sure of how much of the evening Mary-Jane was aware of.

Mary-Jane stopped mid movement, holding her heaped spoon of sugar over her steaming cup of tea. 'Don't be a smart arse, Alice. You've already kept us waiting long enough. Did you decide to make a trip into Galway while you were at it?'

Alice went to speak, but Mary-Jane put up her hand to stop her. 'Either you got the Trophy or you did not.' She glared at Alice.

Alice decided now was not the time to try and tough it out with Mary-Jane. She gave a straight positive answer and chose not to mention anything about Alexandra.

'And have you forgotten anything?' Mary-Jane added.

Alice was confused. What could she have forgotten? 'Sorry, what do you mean?'

'The key?' Mary-Jane whispered through clenched teeth.

'Crikey, yes, the key.' Alice was mortified. How could she have forgotten?

'It is the sort of thing that would be missed by now, don't yaw think?' Mary-Jane added sarcastically. 'Miss Ash would have already gone to unlock the back door.'

Alice felt weak and very stupid. 'Mary-Jane, I forgot completely.' Alice's heart tightened in her chest at the thoughts of any consequences of not returning the key.

She stuttered, trying to explain herself, when Mary-Jane put her hand up again.

'Relax, Alice. Fortunately for us it is a copy. We all would have been in a lot of trouble if we were to rely on you to bring back the only key of the back door, eh?' There were giggles from the other girls at the table.

'The original is where it should be, and no one is any the wiser,' Mary-Jane said with confidence.

Alice smiled nervously, extremely relieved.

'As for the Trophy,' Mary-Jane continued. 'You can give that to me after breakfast. Meet us at the mountain Pokey. Come on your own, no groupies.' Mary-Jane glanced over at Bessie and Gale.

Alice had never been up to the mountain Pokey and was excited at the prospect. But she had to admit that she was nervous about having to do it alone.

CHAPTER 21

Anti-climax

'Make yourselves at home, why don't ye.' Alice threw herself onto what space was left on her bed, having returned from the Pokey to find Gale and Bessie waiting in her cubicle.

'We just want to know how you got on,' Bessie said defensively.

'It was a bit of an anti-climax, really,' Alice sighed.

'What do you mean?' Bessie sat up straight in the bed.

'Well, for one thing, the Pokey isn't exactly the Ritz. Just a bunch of logs circling a lot of mud and fag butts.'

'What were you expecting?' Gale asked. 'Log fires and Mary-Jane toasting marshmallows? Never mind the décor, what happened?'

'Oh, just Mary-Jane and her cronies.' Alice remembered how nice Mary-Jane, Felicity, and Ting had been when she first met them, and promised herself she would not go turn-coat on First Years when she became their senior.

'It was like the whole thing was just so casual. She took the Trophy and basically said it was a job well done, but that it did not guarantee my place on the next raiding of the Ref.'

'What! Are you serious?' Bessie exclaimed. 'After all that and with being locked into the Gothic by Alexandra and all?'

Alice turned and plumped up a pillow.

'You did tell them about Alexandra locking you in, didn't you?' Bessie demanded.

'I sort of left that detail out,' Alice replied sheepishly.

'But why? That good for nothing had it in for you and you didn't say a *word*?' Alice didn't respond, and the silence hung like a heavy cloud in the cubicle.

'Maybe Alice is right, Bessie,' Gale offered. 'I suppose it mightn't do much good.'

'How do you figure that?' Bessie asked, looking from Alice to Gale.

'Alice got herself out of the jam,' Gale explained. 'If Mary-Jane knows about Alexandra locking Alice in, then it proves that Alice is even better than they thought, finding an alternative escape route and having to tell about the trapdoor.'

'Surely that would be a good thing?' Bessie frowned.

'On one hand perhaps, but we don't want Alice proving herself a superhero now, do we? There is no point in turning in Alexandra at this point. Alice would only be seen as a ratter. Although the trouble Alexandra would get into might be worth it?' Gale smiled vindictively at Alice.

Alice shifted on the bed. 'Who's to say whether they know or not. The main thing is that Alexandra and I know, and she knows I got out. How I did it must be killing her, and I am happy that she puzzles over that for a while.'

'I'm not sure I get it,' Bessie clapped her hands together, 'but I am good with letting her stew in it for a while. That girl deserves whatever is coming to her. Whatever that might be.'

Alice tuned out as Bessie argued with Gale about the pros and cons of the seniors knowing about Alexandra. She wasn't so sure of her own brilliance. Feeling paranoid now at who knew what and not being able to tell someone the full story was eating her.

This game of cover-up was confusing, and Alice wished the two girls would go and leave her in peace. Not knowing how or what to say, Alice stood and decided to brush her teeth. She reached for her toothbrush and paste and proceeded to lose herself in the rhythm of her brushing.

'Must brush my own.' Gale stood up and stretched. 'Not long to study. You coming, Bessie?' Gale held back the curtain. 'Meet you down there,' Alice grunted with a mouth full of paste suds. Bessie bounced up next to Gale. 'Yeah, okay, see you down there,' and she skipped out of the cubicle following Gale.

Standing in front of her mirror, Alice looked at the reflection of herself and that of the wall behind her. Spotting something that wasn't right, Alice rinsed and spat, and turned to face her wall. She scanned her collage of postcards and magazine cut-outs that formed a pattern on the wall.

There was an obvious gap where something had once been tacked. One of her postcards was gone. It was one of her favourites, a black and white photo of a couple kissing in Paris. Searching around her bed and pulling it out from the wall, Alice searched for the postcard to no avail. The study bell sounded and, thinking the postcard lost amongst the rest of her stuff shoved under her bed, she promised herself to search properly for it later and promptly forgot about it.

CHAPTER 22

Follow-up with Ruth

'Psst.' Alice jumped when Ruth's head and shoulders appeared through her cubicle wall. 'Crikey, Ruth, I wish you wouldn't do that.'

A giggling Ruth sat up on Alice's dresser. It was some days later, and Alice was getting ready for breakfast

'Where have you been? I have been dying to talk to you.'

Ruth raised her eyebrows at Alice.

'Sorry, you know what I mean. It's just that since the night of the Gothic I haven't been able to talk to anyone. Tanya is playing it cool, as she has to, with me and I have given up even smiling at her as it would appear she doesn't want any acknowledgement from me at all. And Mary-Jane and the guys haven't said anything more about it either. Except for Alex's quiet empty threats of getting me back, it's almost like I was never there.'

Alice started to pick at her duvet. 'What do *you* know? What are the other girls saying? Are the supervisors suspicious?'

'It's all about you, isn't it Alice?' Ruth asked tiredly.

'What?'

'I have spent years hanging around here with no one to talk to, no one to answer any of my questions, no one to be suspicious of me, and you are complaining about a few days?' She glided down from the dresser. Alice looked blankly at her.

'Alice there is more to school and day-to-day stuff here than you and your trip to the Gothic. Did you know that Ana Bamway's mother is dying or that Dame Mary is struggling to keep the school afloat with rising costs? It would be a different matter if you had been left stuck in the Gothic, if you had been caught having gotten a back door key and escaped after curfew, found cold and frightened alone in the Gothic. There would have been great consequences had the outcome been different.'

The reality of what might have happened, only for Ruth, began to dawn on Alice. She hung her head. Ruth was right. She should be grateful to her for her help.

'Consider yourself lucky, Alice. At least you can talk about it with Bessie and Gale. At least you can talk with someone.'

Alice saw tears pool in Ruth's eyes. 'Ruth, I'm sorry. I should've . . .'

'Forget about it, Alice.' Ruth shook her head, composing herself. 'How could you possibly know what it is like for me? I can't explain it to myself, let alone to you.' Ruth moved to leave.

'Look the whole thing will wash over. I've seen it before. There is all this great excitement with the Gothic and the Trophy and then the seniors clamp down on raiding the Ref. It is all a bit of a tease, to be honest.'

Alice didn't understand.

'It is a joke, Alice. Whatever about Alexandra and Tanya — that was bad luck. The Gothic is a gambling opportunity for the seniors, laying bets on whether or not you would make it. Most girls don't even make it out the back door, chickening out at the last minute. Some have made it as far as the other side of the gate. Few make it to the Gothic at all, never mind actually get in. Alexandra had bet on you losing. She lost some money on you.'

Alice couldn't believe what Ruth was telling her. 'Why didn't you say something? Warn me?'

'I guessed you were up for it. I knew you would be able, especially with my help. I was just a bit late in getting to you.

You know what my timing is like. The seniors don't know about Alexandra locking you in, or Tanya. That is your secret. And Alexandra's and Tanya's for their own part.' Alice slumped onto her bed. 'Tanya cannot let on, not because she was out with Paddy John, but because she was caught, and Alexandra will be in deep trouble for trying to fix the bet.' Ruth paced back and forth in front of Alice 'Life will just tick on and the usual routine will kick in for another while until tuck supplies wear thin and raiding the Ref features once again.'

Alice sighed. She had so been looking forward to the excitement of it all, and now life at boarding school seemed all of a bit of a rollercoaster with its short highs and monotonous lows. She would just have to settle in with whatever the seniors would dictate and get on with day-to-day stuff. At least she did have Bessie and Gale.

'Ruth?' Alice called her attention shyly. Ruth had her arms folded and was pouting.

'I am really sorry, Ruth. I don't really know what it must be like for you, so you will have to keep reminding me every so often.'

'I shouldn't have to keep reminding you, Alice. If you were a friend, you should just remember.'

Alice was about to say something when the curtain to her cubicle was tugged aside by Bessie 'Are you two coming to breakfast?' Bessie looked surprised. 'Oh, I thought Gale was here too.' Bessie looked beyond Alice to the empty cubicle. 'Who were you talking to?'

'No one.' Alice tucked her hair up into a ponytail.

'But you were talking . . .' Bessie was interrupted by the arrival of Gale.

'Hey you two, what's up?' Alice stepped forward, forcing Bessie out into the corridor.

'Nothing, Bessie here thinks I have gone mad and have started talking to myself.' Alice thumped Bessie on the back, smiling. 'I wonder if there are some Rice Krispies this morning?' Alice directed the question at Bessie to distract her. 'Do you want some of my hot chocolate to make up your magic milk mix?'

'Yum,' Bessie rubbed her tummy, already thinking about breakfast. 'Just what the doctor ordered'.

CHAPTER 23

Leisure Time with Ruth

The excitement of Alice's Trophy success soon faded, and days passed quickly with the routine of school work and competitive sports. It wasn't long until the Christmas tests, and anticipation of the approaching holidays occupied the students' minds.

Alice found no rhyme or reason to Ruth's comings and goings. There were days when she would not see her at all, and then Ruth would happily turn up again, seeking Alice's company, and Alice, feigning a headache to her other friends, would escape with Ruth for some fresh air and a wander in the grounds.

A favourite spot for both girls was to walk along the old path that led up the south side of Duchruach Mountain, overlooking the old walled garden. Ruth had shown the disused path to Alice, and Alice intentionally had not shared the spot with any other girls, savouring the space and view for herself. Ruth had explained it was the old service path where the pipes were laid to bring water from Lake Toucher to the castle and the gardens below. Some old steps were carved into the hillside here and there, but mostly the path was hidden by overgrowth.

It was so peaceful and quiet up there, from where they could see the valley spread out before them, with a bird's view of the walled gardens below. It was a cold but beautiful December Saturday and this time Alice used the excuse of going for a jog to get away from the rest of the girls. It wouldn't be long before Alice and Ruth would be separated by the school holidays. Finding a good spot on the side of the hill, Alice sat with Ruth as they took in the sights below.

'The walled gardens were the original walled gardens of the castle in the Mitchell Henry days,' Ruth explained. 'There wasn't much of them left even when we were students here, because the next owners, the Manchesters, had let the place go to ruin, and when the nuns bought Kylemore, they found it too much to try and restore them. I suppose it was more practical anyway to use them as vegetable gardens for the Abbey and school.'

Alice shivered as the mountain wind whipped threads of her hair about her. Ruth was a vision of perfection as she was unaffected by the mountain breeze. Nestling deeper into the soft wild growth around her, Alice hugged her knees in tight to her chest. She watched as the workmen, who looked like big ants in the distance below, were busy in the vegetable plots. She could make out the familiar form of Ben, the handyman, and thought she could make out PJ and his son Paddy John. Alice's eyes scanned the overgrown paths and remnants of the rusted skeletal frames of the old conservatory that might have once housed magnificent plants and flowers.

'It must have been very beautiful.'

'Oh yes, even in its time it was considered a feat of great engineering. I think Mitchell Henry must have been influenced by what he saw at the Great Exhibition at Crystal Palace.'

'The what, where? Alice asked.

'1851? Crystal Palace? The world's biggest industrial exhibition hosted by Queen Victoria and Prince Albert?'

Alice shook her head; nothing Ruth was saying rang any history bells for her.

'Never mind,' Ruth said impatiently. 'No doubt you didn't know that the original main road to Clifden passed through where the walled gardens are now?' Ruth paused for effect.

Alice smiled meekly and shrugged her shoulders. 'Henry re-directed the road over the causeway that he had built at the East Gate, and created a whole new road away from the castle. So it would be more private, I suppose, and then they incorporated the old road into the gardens. Converted it into the gravelled walk that is there now.' Ruth pointed it out below them. 'They chose to place the gardens here because it was the hottest and brightest spot near the castle with its lovely south-facing sloped site.'

'Wow. You really do know your stuff, Ruth.' Alice followed the line of the path from the arched entrance gate on the east side of the gardens to the other on the western wall. She smiled, thinking of her mother always saying that a garden should be south-facing for best light and growth.

'The stream cuts the garden in half, dividing it so that there was a flower and vegetable garden; and there were twenty-one glasshouses that were interconnected. They were full of exotic fruits and plants. Henry was very clever, using a system of pipes and boilers to bring heat and water to them.' Ruth pointed out the various areas as she spoke.

Alice tried to imagine how that might have looked, thinking how much her mother would have loved the landscaped gardens.

'I heard once that Dame Veronica tried to tackle the growth and wilderness that had taken over. She was an old Choir Dame, who broke with tradition and worked with the lay sisters in the gardens.'

'A Choir Dame?' Alice imagined someone singing in the garden.

'A Choir Dame was the title they gave to a Benedictine nun who was educated and could read and sing Divine Office. They usually came with a dowry to the order and had a vote in the Abbey. Lay sisters were generally uneducated and so were the manual workers of the community. And they didn't have to have a dowry.'

'I never knew there was that much of a difference between them. I remember Ting saying something before, but didn't realise there were rules about it all.'

'Oh, you don't know the half of it, but that was all done away with by the Second Vatican Council in the sixties. The rules were dispensed with and the title of Sister was given to all.'

'So do you know why Dame Mary is still a Dame?'

'Not officially. Respect, I suppose. Some of the nuns choose to keep the title for some of the older nuns who had been professed before Vatican Two. As they died, their title died with them, newly professed nuns taking on the simple title of Sister.'

'I like the fact that she is still called Dame, I think it suits her.'

Ruth nodded.

Alice smiled at Ruth. 'How do you know all this stuff Ruth?'

'Well, I have lived to see it all, metaphorically speaking, of course.'

'I have heard some bits and pieces from other girls,' Alice said, 'but the details seem to gather legs and arms. Like some girls used to say that Margaret Henry never got to see the completion of the castle, when she did actually get to live here for some years. And then there was talk of Mitchell Henry turning to drink and gambling after she died. But I'm not so sure about that. And not many know of the Manchesters owning the estate. I think some of the girls get mixed up between them. The Henrys sound like they were nice landlords, not sure if the same could be said of the Manchesters. Is it true he treated the Irish workers like slaves?'

'Oh, the gossip doesn't surprise me, Alice,' Ruth replied. 'Even I wonder sometimes what I have picked up over the years.'

'What do you mean?'

'Well take Sister Martin, for example.' Ruth raised her eyebrows questioningly. 'What do you know about her?'

Alice laughed as she adjusted her seat on the side of the mountain.

'Sister Martin? Well, I know she is not a nun to be messed with. I hear that she was the youngest of a very large family and was left in a convent at the age of four as her own parents could not afford to raise her. That she became a kind of daughter to the nuns?' Alice paused, looking to Ruth for correction and, on receiving none, continued. 'They say she went off to train to be a vet, was dumped at the altar, left the outside world and came back to the nuns after some mental breakdown.'

Ruth laughed. 'You have got to be kidding me? Where did you hear *that story*?'

'From the older girls,' Alice answered sheepishly.

'And you believed them?'

'Well what's not to believe?' Alice thought of Sister Martin and her intimidating presence. She walked tall and with confidence, had a commanding voice that was profound and vaguely threatening all at once. Not the serene image one usually has of a nun. Not that Alice had much contact with this nun, avoiding her if at all possible.

'Sister Martin is one of the hardest working nuns in the Abbey,' Ruth said.

'I don't doubt that for a moment,'

'Yes, some nuns raised her, but not these ones. She was the youngest of nine, and her mother died in childbirth. Her father couldn't raise all the children on his own. The Sisters of

Charity raised her as their ward. It was fairly normal in its day. And yes, she was trained as a veterinary surgeon, but nothing untoward or anything bad happened. It was pretty rare for a woman to achieve as much as she did. But apparently she always had the calling to God, and chose the Benedictine Order for reasons only known to herself. She uses her skills with the horses and farm, helping out locals whenever there is any trouble. She commands a lot of respect among the farmers and landowners hereabouts.'

Alice tried to visualise this new side to the impressive nun.

'You should see her when she is with the animals on the farm.' Ruth's eyes strayed into the distance, as if trying to remember something. 'She is so caring and gentle. The farm hasn't changed much at all over the years. Sister Martin still farms by the old traditions.' Ruth's voice trailed off.

'I have a vague memory of being there once. On the farm, that is. When I was alive. I liked the animals, too. I don't think I was there too often, like it was not my place to help out.' Ruth paused trying to remember. 'Of course, it was before Sister Martin's time, but there was someone else there then . . .'

Alice sat up, alert. Ruth's memory would come in patches, and Alice was learning not to interrupt if a thing from the present sparked a memory for her.

'There was another Dame then, I can't remember her name.' Ruth smiled at someone who wasn't there. 'I used to occasionally sneak down to help milk the cows.'

'What's so strange about that?

'I started here in 1923, Alice. The school had only just opened as an Irish finishing school for young ladies. Ladies of society did *not* milk cows,' Ruth said indignantly.

'Oh,' Alice mumbled, embarrassed.

'I think I might even have helped with a cow calving

once.' Ruth paused and frowned. 'I can't remember clearly, it's too cloudy.'

A dull bang sounded from beneath, snapping the girls out of their thoughts. Alice saw that one of the workers had pulled closed the big gates to the walled garden. The two girls watched as Ben and the other workers made their way to a van.

'Ben's nice. I like him.'

'Yes, he is. His father used to work here before him. His dad was John-Joe and his dad before him too. They were all John-Joes till Ben arrived. They called Ben after the nuns, you know as in Benedict.' Ruth smiled again at another memory and then paused, trying to remember the details.

'Why are you smiling?'

'Not sure myself, I remember his father was a nice gentle soul. Kind, polite. I feel connected to him and, as a result, to Ben, but cannot explain why.'

Alice shrugged her shoulder, accepting yet another fuzzy memory of Ruth's.

'We'd better start heading back, Ruth, it's getting dark and, whatever about you, I need to get back for the call to study.' Alice stood up, wiping down her skirt and pulling her coat tightly around her. 'Ruth, if it helps at all, I am sure your memory will come back to you. Just give it some time.'

'Time is certainly something I have plenty of,' Ruth said miserably as she floated past Alice and started to head down the mountain.

★★★

Alice had been having regular enough contact from home by letter and a weekly phone call. She had finally gotten used to the old wind-up phone and operator system, ringing home usually on a Sunday. Betty who lived at the post office was a gentle old soul who would happily connect the girls who wanted to reverse the charges. But Alice's parents had never been much for telephone chitchat or letter writing, and so conversations were short and stilted. Alice certainly wasn't going into details of her adventures. Pete, on the other hand, had been fairly good at keeping in touch. Alice enjoyed getting his letters. Alice had received letters from some relations wishing her well when she first started in boarding school and some from old friends, but Pete had been the most loyal, sending her snippets of this and that, funny stories or even the odd small treat of stickers or funny postcards. His contact was a reminder that there was a world beyond boarding school, which she welcomed when she felt the odd pang of homesickness or was caught up in the politics of the school.

Letters were a constant source of gossip, news, love and a taste of home that school could never offer. And the quantity of post received in a day ranked the popularity status of a girl among the other students. Seniors would receive post daily from their network of family and friends, or even boyfriends, a keen strategy having been meticulously implemented so that they had a constant flow of mail. New girls and First Years soon realised the importance of that contact from the outside world, but it would take several months and even years to have a system in place to guarantee a daily flow of plentiful mail. Some even organised pen pal clubs to increase their chances of getting a daily letter. Anything to have contact with the outside world.

As the holidays approached, the quantity of letters into the school decreased as friends and relatives held back to give their news in person. The night before departure, Alice had packed up and was finding it very difficult to get to sleep with the excitement. Ruth appeared in Alice's cubicle and was feeling sad that she would be alone again. Alice reassured her that the time passing would be like a second in Ruth's time.

Any girls that were not picked up directly from school travelled by private bus to Galway. There the girls were met by parents or took the train home to Dublin or on to other parts of the country. Alice enjoyed the train journey from Galway. The Kylemore girls occupied at least two carriages and there was great banter and antics. Alice would have to say her goodbyes at Portarlington to take the Cork train, which was a much older train with stale old carriages, tacky upholstery and an uninviting dining car.

To say she was disappointed that she was not met in Cork by either of her parents was putting it mildly. Despite the fact that her father had written to say that he would meet her, Alice was surprised to see his secretary there to greet her off the train. But her bad humour soon evaporated on getting home, melted by a warm hug from her mother. She spent an obligatory twenty four hours at home, sleeping in, catching up and helping with Christmas decorations and dressing the Christmas tree. Family responsibility fulfilled, Alice was guilt free in getting on with the more important things in her life.

She was very excited to see Pete and catch up with the news of school and what others classmates had gotten up to. There were only a few days before Christmas Day, and so they made the most of what time they had, hanging out together in the forest.

CHAPTER 24

Christmas

It was Christmas Day and the family had followed their usual tradition of Mass and then Alice's parents having drinks with neighbours. Alice had kept an eye out at Mass for Pete, but his family never showed up. She presumed that they had gone to a different one. Finally she was distracted by Christmas dinner, followed by the family present giving.

Santa no longer visited the Stone household, and she missed the excitement of his pending arrival. Alice had made a big effort to find things for her family and was secretly hoping for gifts that would make returning to boarding school special. Perhaps some cool posters, a new ghetto-blaster or radio, maybe even a Walkman with some tapes of the latest *Top of The Pops* chart hits.

After a late dinner, they sat around the Christmas tree, her parents with post-dinner drinks, Alice and her siblings with fizzy drinks, as each parcel was gifted one at a time.

'It's for when you are cold, you know, in school.' Alice's mum was disappointed at the unenthusiastic reaction to her Christmas gift for Alice. 'You *had* been complaining how cold it can be.'

Alice looked from the old quilt that lay folded on her lap back to her mother. 'I know mum, but this, this is . . .' Alice couldn't finish her sentence. There wasn't anything she could say that would not sound ungrateful or complaining. 'Isn't this an antique?' She smiled weakly at her parents.

'That's the way to look at it, my girl.' Alice's dad encouraged.

'Indeed, you could call it a relic,' Alice's brother mocked.

He chuckled at his own joke. Alice's dad winked at her.

'Ignore Michael,' Alice's mum said. 'Yes, I suppose you could say it is an antique. After all it was your grandmother's, God rest her. She used to say that whoever slept with it would sleep pleasant dreams. She made it herself, you know.'

'Yes Mum, I know. You told us when you offered the quilt to Christine last year.' Alice's sister, on hearing her name, looked up from her new book. 'Huh, oh yeah, the quilt, good luck with that Alice.' She then added teasingly, 'How does the story go again, Mum, I don't think you have ever told us that one.' Alice's mum made a face at Christine and was about to re-tell the familiar story when Alice interrupted.

'Granny saved any scraps of material and spent many months slowly working the squares together. And then it was passed on in turn to you, Mum. What was it she used to say?' And knowing the story so well, the rest of the family all pitched in with the family clichéd chant, '*There has been a whole lot of love sewn into that quilt.*' They all laughed.

'Are you sure, Mum? I'd hate if something happened to it at school.' Alice struggled to think of another excuse.

'Well, it's not going to see much light here, that's for sure. I had put it safely away until you were old enough to pass it on to. And then your sister rejected it.' Alice's mum glanced over at Christine. 'I thought it was time I try passing it on to you, Alice.' Alice's mum went quiet. 'I was delighted to get it from my mum. You are so like her, Alice.' Alice looked sadly at her mother.

'Now enough of that talk, whose next for a present?' and Alice's mum retrieved another present from under the tree.

Later, Alice weighed up her Christmas day. On balance it had been good, there hadn't been any major arguments, not with her siblings anyway. Hardly a day would go by and there would be some cross words between them. They were happy to leave her watch the telly with her mum and dad as they escaped to their own rooms with their records and presents. But Alice was disappointed in general with her Christmas stash. A game of Scrabble, an Aran jumper, the quilt and a few other trinkets from her siblings. There wasn't much to be bragging about. Her mum had really taken on her complaints about school to heart, thinking the jumper and quilt would keep her warm, and the Scrabble to give her something to play with her friends in the evenings. Alice ran her hands over the quilt; it was pretty but old looking, and there was a smell of mothballs off it.

There was no way Alice was going to put this on display on her bed. She felt she was already the butt of some senior jokes because of her hand-me-down duvet covers and she was not going to draw any more attention to herself by displaying some smelly old thing. She would never hear the end of it. Alexandra would have a field day with it. Of all the cubicles in the dorm, Alexandra's had all the latest with posters of Billy Idol, Kim Wilde and Culture Club, and she was forever playing up-to-date tapes on her new ghetto blaster. God only knows what she would be bringing back with her after the Christmas holidays. Alice imagined her with so much new kit that she would probably be doing a full re-decoration of her cubicle.

Alice stroked the patchworks and decided that she would bring it to school, so as not to upset her mother, but she would have to keep it hidden under her bed.

CHAPTER 25

Quick Stop

The last days of the holidays passed slowly for Alice. Part of her really looked forward to going back to school, and another part of her wanted to stay at home.

But now her bags were packed and there were no more days left. Alice jumped into the back seat of the car.

'Ready to go?' Alice's mum asked, leaning back over the passenger seat. Her parents were dropping her back to the train, and Alice was grateful for that at least.

'As ready as I will ever be, I suppose.'

Alice's dad pulled out of the drive and began the journey quietly. Taking the quiet back road towards the city, Alice knew they would be passing Pete's house on the way. The car slowed as they approached the entrance.

Alice sat upright in her back seat. 'Oh, are we stopping at Pete's to say goodbye?

'I have to return some platters to Pete's mum that I borrowed over Christmas anyway, thought you might like to say goodbye at the same time.'

Mr Stone toot-tooted the horn of the car as they entered the driveway.

The front door of Pete's house opened, and Pete stood looking out. He beamed a smile and waved happily when he recognised the car. Alice watched as he turned and said something to someone behind him in the hall. Sally, his gran, shuffled forward using a walking stick as support. Alice liked Sally; she had lived with Pete and his mum for years and was a great old character with her stories of the Ireland past and all her old sayings, like 'An empty sack won't stand, but a full one won't bend'. Alice was pleased to see her up and about, as she so often just sat in her chair mumbling to herself. Alice got out of the car to go to her. Alice's mum greeted Pete and Sally casually and went on into the house with the dishes. Mr Stone started to turn the car in the drive.

'You've a lot of gear there,' Pete nodded towards the boot crammed with bags 'Yeah,' Alice faltered and looked beyond Pete to the front door of the house. Pete's Gran was determined to make it out to them.

'Hello Sally, how are you to-day?' Alice stepped round Pete and walked to meet the shuffling woman.

'Fine, just fine my dear. Sure you know it will take a silver bullet to get rid of me.'

Alice smiled warmly at her.

'All ready for school, Alice?' Sally stopped to catch her breath and watched the manoeuvring of the car.

'Just about,' Alice said, 'the holidays are never quite long enough. But I am looking forward to getting back and catching up with my friends.'

'Uh, thanks a lot.' Pete gave Alice a friendly shove. Alice shoved him back.

'No doubt you have made some nice new friends there.' Sally shifted her weight. The old woman's eyes held Alice's for a moment, staring intently. Ruth came to mind, and Alice smiled at the thought of seeing her again.

'Some perhaps more interesting than others?' the old woman asked curiously.

Alice laughed inwardly. 'Yes, you could say that.' She enjoyed the quick memory of the misadventures she had with Ruth. Then Alexandra came to mind, and Alice felt a sense strong dislike for the girl.

'Hmm.' Sally stared intently at Alice and something passed between them. Alice suddenly felt uncomfortable and now it was her turn to shift her weight. Alice wondered if there could be truth to Sally having a sixth sense. Pete would often joke fondly that she was just a crazy old woman, but Alice found her annual Halloween parlour games of leaf-reading and fortune-telling eerily intriguing.

Alice was startled at the beeping of the car horn. She laughed at herself.

Sally watched Alice intensely, and then her face broke into a happy, wrinkled smile. 'Mind how you go now, Alice.' Sally opened her arm outwards for a hug. Alice gently embraced her small frame. 'Don't let that Alexandra get you down. There is good in every one, you know.'

Alice was surprised at Sally's reference to the fiery redhead. She had never shared any of her experiences with Sally. Alice guessed Pete must have told her and wondered what else he might have said. Feeling somewhat annoyed that Pete might betray her trust, Alice glared at Pete.

There was an awkward silence.

'Come on, love, we will miss your train,' Alice's dad called out the car window. Alice's mum had returned to the car and was waving goodbye to Sally and Pete.

Alice hesitated at first and then stepped towards Pete, giving him a quick hug. 'I can't believe you told Sally all about Alexandra,' Alice whispered in his ear.

'Huh, what?' Pete looked surprised as Alice pulled away. 'I never did.'

But Alice was gone, jumping back into the car. Alice waved as the car pulled out of the driveway. A confused-looking Pete waved back. Sally stood expressionlessly at his side, the beginnings of a smirk held in the corner of her mouth.

CHAPTER 26

Chicken

Once back in school, the girls showed off their Christmas presents, talked of ski or sun holidays taken abroad, and gossiped about who had done what with whom over the holidays.

Then the days slowed down, wore into weeks, and routine set in. The weather worsened; a damp cold crept into the school as the castle walls retained a fraction of the heat given off by the old radiators. The homework intensified, and the nights got longer and more boring. The girls' timetable was a cycle of classes, sports, study, meals, Mass and Benediction. Ruth came and went, and Alice found it more and more difficult meet her privately. The only free time was that short half hour or so before lights out. Weekends varied slightly, but Bessie and Gale were never far away, opting to hang out in Alice's cubicle chatting and thinking up new ideas to distract themselves.

'If only it wasn't so cold,' Bessie groaned miserably, pulling up her thick woollen socks closer to her knees, 'life would be a bit more bearable.'

'You'd think they would put on the heating more often considering the fees we are paying.' Gale blew into her new fingerless gloves. Bessie had eyed them enviously when Gale showed them off, never having got replacement ones for her lost pair. Gale had fared well with her presents, her mother going over the top lavishing her with all the latest in fashion, music and posters. Gale's cubicle now looked like a private shrine to Madonna. She still didn't like people in her cubicle touching her stuff.

'Two hot water bottles isn't even enough to keep me warm.' Gale adjusted the bottle she was sitting on.

Alice's thoughts turned to the quilt still stuffed in her bag, under her bed. She would like its comforting heat now, but thinking about Gale's new duvet cover and Bessie's super-new heavy-tog sleeping bag made her reconsider. 'Anyone for Scrabble?' Alice asked half jokingly

Bessie and Gale looked up at her with disgust.

'I'm going to make myself some noodles, anyone for some?' Alice pulled out her tuck bag from under her sink.

Alice had given up hiding her stash ages ago, as Gale and Bessie spent so much time in her cubicle – although she did like to keep a couple of bars hidden for when she settled down alone for the night, teasing Ruth with memories of the squares of Cadburys milk chocolate or the long tendrils of caramel from the Highland Toffee.

Alice saw there was only one packet of pot noodles left. In fact her tuck bag was looking pretty dismal. 'Slim pickings I'm afraid, girls,' Alice sighed. 'Only one pack left.'

'And I ate the last of mine last night.' Bessie looked up, realising that she had admitted to eating even more after leaving the girls to go to bed. Gale and Alice stared at her unblinking. 'What? I got hungry again. Okay!' she pulled at her jumper..

'Don't worry, Bessie,' Gale said. I'm eating more too I'm so depressed. The pounds are creeping on.' Gale patted her flat tummy. And then her eyes sparkled mischievously. 'I think it is time the Ref was paid a visit.' Gale waited a second and then added. 'So when are you going to raid the Ref, Alice?'

Alice felt her stomach lurch.

'Are you asking out of hunger or boredom?' Alice pretended that she wasn't bothered and proceeded to open her pack of noodles, breaking them into her mug.

134

'Both.'

'Oh, what a great idea,' Bessie said excitedly.

'Huh, maybe for you, you would get to reap the benefits. And I risk getting expelled. I'm not so sure I want to raid the Ref at all.'

'Ah, come on. Mary-Jane said she would bring you down this term, why not tonight?'

'Cos I have my noodles and I don't mind sharing them with you.'

'We'll go and find Mary-Jane, see if she is game,' Gale declared teasingly. Standing up she began to pull Alice by her jumper. Bessie giggled, enjoying the game. She joined in. 'Oh come on, Alice, it has been so boring lately, give us something to get excited about.'

'No.' Alice pulled away from them.

'Chicken,' Gale teased her.

'Am not.'

'Bawk Bawk Bawk.' Gale flapped her arms.

'Not funny. Stop! No, I don't want to raid the Ref.'

Bessie took up the chicken dance with Gale and the two squawked out into the dormitory corridor, dancing and scratching chicken-like outside Alice's cubicle. Their clucking and antics started to draw attention from the other girls. Curtains were pulled back, bodies leaning out of gaps.

'Stop it,' Alice demanded, looking up and down the corridor at the gathering girls who laughed at Gale and Bessie.

'*Alice is a chick-en, Alice is a chick-en,*' Gale taunted flapping around her.

Alice was getting mad. 'Don't be such a cow, Gale. Bessie, please stop,'

'We're not cows, we're Alice, Alice the chicken.' Gale was laughing.

None of the girls noticed that Alexandra had joined the

crowd. She crossed her arms and smirked at the scene before her. Alice saw her and was furious.

'I told Mary-Jane you would be too scared to go into the Enclosure. You haven't the guts, Alice Stone,' Alexandra mocked.

Alice turned, now furious, towards Alexandra. '*You* of all people should know better, Alexandra. I am NOT too chicken to go into the Enclosure. I can easily find my way in and out, simple as. Just try me'

'Oh really?' Alexandra looked smugly at Alice. Bessie and Gale stopped squawking and stared at the two girls sizing up to each other. Alexandra stood nearly a full head and shoulders over Alice, her backcombed red hair a halo of arrogance and contempt.

'I don't need anyone – not you, not Mary-Jane, and certainly not any of her stupid cronies,' Alice shouted.

Everyone went silent. Alice smiled triumphantly at Bessie and Gale, and then her smile dropped on seeing their pale, staring faces. Bessie nodded to somewhere behind Alice. Alice knew instinctively she had said too much. With dread, Alice turned slowly to find Mary-Jane, Ting and Felicity standing with arms crossed and eyes locked on Alice.

'So, you think you can do it alone, eh Just Billy? Well I would love to see you try. What do you think, girls?' Mary-Jane engaged the onlookers. There were some rushed whispers and muttering.

'Well?' Mary-Jane taunted.

Alice was mortified. Scanning the crowd, she noticed that Bessie looked terrified and Gale stared back at her blankly. Then a voice emerged from the silence.

'Take them on Alice, you can do it.'

Nobody else heard the voice of Ruth as she walked through Alexandra and stood by Alice. Alice felt some strength creep back into her. She glared at Mary-Jane.

'Okay, you're on. I'll raid the Ref. I'll go alone and I'll do it tonight.' Ruth winked encouragingly at Alice.

'And by the way, call me Just Billy if you want, but there is one thing you CAN'T call me, and that is chicken.'

CHAPTER 27

With Ruth in the Ref

Ruth appeared just as Bessie and Gale had been given last warnings by Miss Ash.

'Girls, I will give you detention and have you cleaning toilets for a week if you do not go back to your own cubicles and get to sleep.'

Bessie and Gale were gone in a flash, whispering good luck to Alice.

'What have I done?' Alice whispered to Ruth when they were finally alone.

'But what can go wrong if I am with you? I think the idea is brilliant, we should have thought of it ages ago.' Ruth was sitting on the stool by Alice's head as she lay on her bed. 'Not that I am going to benefit from any of the treats, but I have to admit I am looking forward to sharing in the adventure.'

'Not sure where you think the sharing is. After all, it will be me who has to do the sneaking and will suffer the consequences if I get caught, worse still, find nothing.'

'But that is the best part, you can't get lost, not with me, and you won't get caught with me looking out for you.' Alice couldn't help but be persuaded. And rather than take a chance on Ruth meeting up with her later, Alice convinced her not to leave her side till it was over so that they could be sure she would not vanish into her own realm and miss the whole thing.

The dorm soon settled for the night. Alice was waiting for Mary-Jane to take her as far as the Enclosure. Ruth had gone out to the corridor to check on Miss Ash's movements. Alice jumped when the curtain moved and Tanya snuck in quietly.

Alice was surprised to see her as she had hardly any contact with Tanya since the night of the Gothic.

'You sure you want to go ahead with this? You still have time to back out, you know.' Tanya stood close to the curtain listening for the sound of footsteps, pulling back a fraction to keep a look out.

'What, and have to live that down with Alexandra and the rest of the school, no way.' Alice was surprised at the sound of her own confident voice. She liked the idea of being able to prove herself, even if she did need Ruth to help her.

'You've got guts, that's for sure,' Tanya whispered. 'To go down to the Ref without a guide, well it's a bit mad to be honest, Alice. Here take this route plan.' Tanya shoved a tiny piece of paper with a roughly sketched map of where to go in the Enclosure. 'The corridors are tricky, but if you keep your wits about you, you won't get lost.' Tanya glanced out a slit in the curtain.

'I can't hang around – Mary-Jane is due any minute. Take this too. You will need it when you come to the dry store.' Tanya handed Alice a small teaspoon and was gone before Alice could ask what it was for.

Ruth had reappeared, and Alice showed her the map and the teaspoon.

'We won't need the map, and whatever is the spoon for?'

'Beats me, but if Tanya says I need it I believe her.' Alice had just tucked it into her dressing gown pocket when Mary-Jane pulled open her cubicle curtain.

'Time to go.' Mary-Jane slipped back out again.

Ruth clapped her hands in excitement. They made their way quietly down the stairs, past the lower dorm and down towards the back door. Taking the key from her pocket, Mary-Jane unlocked it and let Alice down the steps into the dark back yard. She stopped and nodded at a small kitchen window that separated the girls from the Enclosure. The top window was titled open.

Checking that the passage was clear, Mary-Jane said, 'This is where I leave you, Alice. I would wish you luck, but I think you will need more than that.' Mary-Jane sneered at Alice.

'That's okay, I have my own guardian angel.' Alice looked at Ruth.

'Whatever.' Mary-Jane waited for Alice to make a move. 'Well go on. You have to climb in the window. You are on your own from there. You have less than an hour before Ash will do her rounds and double-check the back door. You'd better be back before then, or you will be locked out. There's no key in it for you this time.'

'Come on, Alice, the coast is clear.' Ruth had stuck her head in through the wall and back out again. Alice had to stop herself from smiling.

'Thanks, Mary-Jane, I've got it from here,' Alice said. Climbing up onto the window ledge and slipping in through the small gap, Alice left Mary-Jane puzzling over Alice's confidence.

★★★

'Oh, that was so cool. Ruth, this is great. You were right, we should have done this ages ago.'

'Shush, whatever about me, you can't talk normally down here.'

Alice suddenly clasped her hand over her mouth, remembering where she was. She couldn't believe it. She was actually standing in the Enclosure.

A soft dark stillness enveloped them. Everything was different; the walls were brighter, cleaner, and everything had a tidy feel to it. Ruth led the way as Alice blindly groped behind her; they whispered as they went.

'It's not so scary down here. I thought it would be more . . .' Alice struggled to find the word. Ruth suddenly came to a stop and froze with her finger to her lips. Someone was coming. Alice's breath caught in her throat. She stared at Ruth, pleading with her eyes as to what to do. Ruth glanced around her and gestured to Alice to follow. Just in front of them was a tiny cupboard. Alice gently opened the door and stepped inside. She clung to the door to keep it closed, wishing herself invisible. Peering out a gap in the door, Alice was surprised to see Sister Valentine make her way quietly down the corridor. She paused just outside where Alice was hidden while Ruth watched on in dread. Sister Valentine checked herself in front of a decorative mirror that hung beside the Enclosure door. Alice's fingers ached, she wished Ruth could do something to distract the nun. Sister Valentine was still studying herself in the mirror. Alice was trying to make sense of the delay when Ruth suddenly appeared beside her laughing. 'You should see her, she is plucking her eyebrows.'

'What?' Alice mouthed increduoulsy.

'There isn't great light in their quarters. The corridor light here must be better for her private vanities.'

'Oh for God's sake,' Alice thought to herself and rolled her eyes.

'Can't you get rid of her?' Alice mouthed.

'I'll try, but don't depend on it.' And Ruth was gone.

The door to the Enclosure rattled near Sister Valentine. Alice could feel her heart beat madly in her chest. Moving towards the door slowly, Sister Valentine opened it, stepping out into the main corridor, calling gently, 'Is someone there?'

Alice could see Ruth standing behind Sister Valentine and blowing at her neck. Shivering, Sister Valentine blessed herself and quickly shut the door again. She scurried back along the corridor towards the nuns' quarters. Ruth made sure the coast was clear before giving Alice the okay.

'That was close. Come on, let's get this over with.' Ruth quickly led Alice down through the maze of short corridors that twisted and turned in the Enclosure. Alice's sense of direction was all over the place when she realised she was way into the service area of the kitchen. 'Where is the dry store?' Alice had been told by Mary-Jane to bring something back from the dry store as this was where the nuns kept anything worthwhile.

'Oh great!' Alice exclaimed, understanding now why Mary-Jane had put her up to taking something from the dry store. Alice looked at the bolt and padlock securing the door.

'I don't understand.' Ruth looked at Alice.

'Mary-Jane knew the door would be padlocked. If I cannot retrieve anything from the dry store, I don't have proof of a successful raid, and if I don't have proof of a raid I might as well not come down here at all as no-one will believe that I made it.'

'Couldn't you take something else?' Ruth was looking at the vegetables that lay stacked in a basket in the corner.

'Nah, sure I could just have easily picked them up at the back kitchen where the big sacks are stored. No, it has to be something from in here.'

'Oh,' Ruth sighed and disappeared in through the wall of the dry store, only to reappear again. 'I can see why, there is some really good stuff in there' she added teasingly.

'Thanks for that.' A disgruntled Alice slumped down on the step opposite and put her head in her hands. 'Now what will I do?'

Ruth sat down beside her.

'We are running out of time.' Alice frowned checking her watch. 'We have to get back before Miss Ash does her rounds.'

Alice could feel a draught creep around. Plunging her hands for warmth into her dressing gown pockets she felt the spoon that Tanya had given her. Alice took it out and looked at it. Turning it in her hand, Alice looked from the spoon to the dry store and back to the spoon again.

'What did she expect you to do with that, dig your way in?' Ruth asked.

Alice pondered a moment and then suddenly darted to the door.

'Of course! Tanya, you are a genius!'

A puzzled Ruth watched as Alice inspected the door frame.

'The door is only loosely hung by these old hinges. Look at the screws, the paint has been worn off them compared to the rest of the door. Someone has unscrewed them before.' Alice took the spoon and, holding it by the bowl end, she inserted the flat handle tip into the head of the screw and turned. 'It's taking hold!' Slowly Alice undid the screws and, balancing the door carefully, swung it back using the padlock as the swivel point. 'Thank you, Tanya!' Alice beamed at Ruth. 'We're in,' and she slipped inside.

The small room was lined with shelves stacked with all sorts of goods ranging from the boring bags of flour and tins of treacle to the lush supply of biscuits and packets of cakes. Homemade tarts were draped with tea-towels and there were tins of biscuits and homemade scones. Alice didn't know where to start. She felt like she had found Aladdin's cave.

'This is amazing. I had no idea the nuns had it so good. And I thought they took a vow of poverty.'

Alice scanned the shelves, weighing up what could she take that would not be missed. Then she noticed recycled ice cream boxes stacked in the corner of the store. Alice took one down and opened it to find some homemade cookies. 'What do you think?' Alice looked to Ruth.

'Well an ice-cream box filled with home-made cookies is a real dry store giveaway. I think Mary-Jane should be pretty convinced.'

'That's decided then.' Alice took one of the boxes and, placing another tin of biscuits where the box had been, she stepped back and scanned the shelf.

'At a quick glance, everything would look the same.'

'Come on, we better head back.'

After some difficulty Alice managed to screw the door back on its hinges.

Alice was tired but elated by the time they had made their way back along the corridor, relying on Ruth to give her the clearance to move quickly around corners and back up out of the Enclosure. Alice found herself in a different part of the castle, the corridor that led up to the church, and was genuinely confused as to how Ruth had brought her to this point. Leading Alice through the small chapel, Ruth brought Alice through the back door into another hidden corridor, and in a jiffy had them both back on the main stairs that led them to the Big Dorm. Alice was impressed.

'Alice, there is no end to the back corridors and secret passageways in this old place. Believe you me, I came across them all when exploring the old castle walls.'

Alice was intrigued but anxious to get back. Nervous that Ash might be making one of her random rounds, they made their way quickly back up to the Big Dorm. There was a moment when they had to wait for a prefect to come back from the washrooms, but otherwise the return had been plain sailing. Alice was about to head around to Mary-Jane's cubicle when she recognised the footfall of an approaching Miss Ash. She nipped into her own cubicle. Alice accepted that she would have to wait again until the morning before she could hand over her proof to Mary-Jane.

Tucking the box under her sink, she climbed into bed, exhausted. 'Thanks again, Ruth, gosh that *was* fun.' Alice yawned. 'I loved catching Sister Valentine pruning herself. I always suspected that she was a tad vain.' Alice smiled a sleepy smile and burrowed further under her covers.

'My pleasure,' Ruth giggled, 'But I think you mean preening herself'.

'Huh?' Alice yawned, not paying attention. 'Night, Ruth. Try and stay around for the fun and games tomorrow.' She turned in towards the wall and settled in for the night.

'I certainly hope to,' replied Ruth, but Alice was already asleep.

CHAPTER 28

After Raiding the Ref

Alice woke early after a fretful night's sleep, feeling groggy and tired. Ruth was already sitting at the end of her bed smiling. Soon the raucous call of Miss Ash could be heard at the lower dorm, and stirrings in the other cubicles soon followed. Alice then decided to make her way over to the senior side of the dorm and to Mary-Jane's cubicle. Tapping on the partition, Alice waited for a grunt of permission from Mary-Jane before entering.

Mary-Jane's cubicle was like a shrine to all things pop and modern. Every inch of wall space was crammed with posters, postcards and photos from the three years that Mary-Jane had spent at Kylemore. Magazine cut-outs filled any small gaps between posters of Jim Morrison, Mickey Rourke and Garfield. Alice stared at the lump that stirred under the Wham duvet heaped full of stuffed toys and a giant teddy bear.

'Mary-Jane?' Alice whispered. A muffled moan could be heard from under the duvet. Alice looked to Ruth, who simply shrugged her shoulders.

'Mary-Jane, it's Alice.'

'What? Oh, yeah.' A head of spaghetti hair and squinting, tired eyes appeared.

'So how did you get on?' Mary-Jane dragged herself up into a sitting position, rubbing the sleep from her face and dragging at her hair.

Ruth giggled. Alice tried not to smile at the Paddington pyjamas Mary-Jane was wearing.

'Great,' Alice replied triumphantly.

Mary-Jane stopped mid a wake-up stretch. 'What?'

'Yeah, it was easy-peasy. Had to think my way around the dry store, but got in and have something for you.' Alice handed Mary-Jane the old ice-cream tub with the cookies. Mary-Jane straightened in her bed.

'Well, I'll be damned.' She looked up at Alice. 'I don't know how you do it, Just-Billy, but you just keep coming up trumps. I take my hat off to you.' Mary-Jane scratched her head. 'D'ya know it took me till the end of second year to figure out the dry store, after several failed attempts at sneaking around the Enclosure. Some of those nuns like to stay up pretty late.' Mary-Jane stood out of the bed and stretched again.

Alice started to laugh. 'Yeah, we, I mean I, came across Sister Valentine, but I hid in the hall cupboard.'

Mary-Jane didn't notice Alice's slip; she was at her sink, splashing water on her face. 'Valentine, eh? Yeah, she is a bit of a silent mover. Hard to hear her coming. But normally it is Martin that likes to hang around late, usually out checking on the animals or something. You never know with her. Whatever about the day time, you do not cross Martin after Compline.' Mary-Jane patted her face dry with a pretty towel anagrammed with an elaborate embroidered 'M J' on it.

'I know,' Alice agreed. 'So what happens now?'

'Oh, not much, I simply hold onto the cookies and report back to *my* seniors. You get to keep your chin up.'

'Oh.'

Mary-Jane stood and looked at Alice's sad face 'Hey, you did good, Just-Billy. Take some of these for your buddies – at least you will have some proof of your adventure.' Mary-Jane handed Alice some cookies. Reluctantly Alice took them. Mary-Jane had started to pull off her pyjama bottoms and then stalled, giving Alice a 'get out of here' look.

'Is that it?' Ruth asked Alice as she made her way around to the junior side of the dorm. Alice looked at Ruth, shrugged her shoulders and whispered, 'Suppose so.'

Walking around the corner, Alice came face to face with Alexandra. 'Talking to yourself again, Alice? Going mad after a failed Ref raiding, I suppose.'

'You can suppose away, Alexandra.' Alice held up a cookie and took a teasingly slow bite, not taking her eyes off Alexandra as she did. Surprised at the bitterness of the cookie, Alice pretended it was delicious and made the appropriate yummy sounds. Alexandra stared at Alice's hand, beyond to Mary-Jane's cubicle and back to the cookie. She opened her mouth in surprise.

Alice held her head high and strode past Alexandra, saying no more and swallowing with difficulty what was left in her mouth.

★★★

Bessie was waving madly at Alice as she came down the stairs to breakfast. Whispering and nudges passed among the girls as the gossip started up of what might have happened the night before.

'Tell me everything?' Bessie demanded when Alice found her seat. 'Shush.' Alice did not want an audience. 'Gimme a sec.' Alice paused. 'Where's Gale?'

'Oh, she had to go to the toilet,' Bessie explained. Just then Gale appeared at the Ref door.

'So how did last night go?' Gale asked breathlessly, throwing a leg over the bench.

Alice recounted the story in whispers, and they giggled when she told them about Sister Valentine.

'I knew she had to be plucking. Those brows are way too neat to be natural,' Bessie tutted.

Gale was about to say something when there was a loud bang as the door from the kitchen Enclosure slammed open and Sister Martin stormed into the Refectory. Benches were shoved back noisily as girls stood quickly to attention. Everyone stared at the fuming nun. Alice nearly fainted as she recognised the old ice-cream tub that Sister Martin held up for all to see.

'Who has stolen my cookies?' Sister Martin stood at the top of the Ref, holding the tub in the air.

Bessie and Gale looked at Alice. Alice didn't move, just kept staring ahead wide-eyed, looking at the tub that Sister Martin now waved in the air.

'They were all there last night. Someone entered the Enclosure, broke in and stole a tub just like this one from the dry store. Whoever you are, you are a thief. I want to know who it is.'

Silence. A teaspoon fell somewhere in the Ref.

'Right, if that is the way it is going to be, there will be no post until whoever is responsible owns up and returns the cookies.' There were some muffled grumbles and complaints. Knowing, blaming eyes looked to Alice. Alice was afraid to look at anyone.

Dame Mary slowly walked into the Ref and stood by Sister Martin's side. She looked at the ashen faces of the girls before her. Sister Martin looked at Dame Mary and back at the girls, announcing, 'Right, that's that then', and she stormed out.

The girls remained standing. Dame Mary simply shook her head silently.

'Girls, I am so disappointed. As much for yourselves as for Sister Martin. Today is Sister Martin's birthday. She had baked the cookies herself to share with the community. I would ask whoever is responsible to own up and, if it makes it easier,

149

they can come to me in private. I will be in my office till the class bell rings. You have until then.' With that, Dame Mary turned and left.

The Ref burst into objections and catcalls. Alice didn't know where to look. 'Come on Alice, I think we better get out of here.' Bessie was tugging on Alice's sleeve. Alice hesitated. Looking around the Ref, she made eye contact with Mary-Jane who had made it down in time for the whole debacle. Mary-Jane stared at Alice. Alice considered going over to the senior table, but decided against it. She started to make her way out of the Ref.

Alexandra glared smugly at Alice. 'Not so cocky now, are we?' she sneered.

The other girls at her table looked from Alice to Alexandra and a murmuring of gossip took up, quickly passing from table to table. Alice just stood there as the girls looked on, darting evil eyes at her, but no one actually said anything. There was a code after all. No ratting. But that didn't mean there wasn't a great heat off those that wished they could. Especially Alexandra.

'Best we keep moving,' Bessie encouraged, and the three girls made their way back up to the dorm.

'No post! I don't believe it.' Bessie was disgusted.

'The Sixth Years won't stand for it, that is for sure,' Gale added.

Alice was muddling over the problem of having to confess and didn't understand. 'What do you mean?'

'It's Valentine's Day on Monday.'

'Oh, my *God*,' Bessie squirmed.

'The whole school will be furious,' Gale added.

Valentine's Day, the busiest postal day in the entire year, when getting a letter proved that a girl was popular, admired, loved or sought after. Of course, amongst love letters and

Valentine cards were regular letters from parents or grandparents. But this did not matter come lunchtime when Miss Ash would stand with the basket of mail and call out girls' names. To receive any mail on Valentine's Day was a bonus, and for those who did not, well they would leave the Ref with heavy hearts in the hope that the next day would bring yearnings from some lovesick admirer.

'Surely it's illegal? It must be against the law to withhold private mail. That or at least it goes against our human rights.' Gale was not happy; she was hoping to get some mail from her mother at least.

'How could I have been so stupid? I mean of all the biscuits to take, they had to be Martin's. I should have just taken a packet of Kimberleys.'

'But anyone could have a packet of Kimberleys,' Bessie said. 'No, you made a good choice taking the homemade ones, it's just a shame that they had to be Martin's.'

It wasn't long before Mary-Jane appeared at Alice's curtain, agitated and out of breath.

'Alice, can I have a word?'

Alice stepped out into the corridor and followed Mary-Jane around to her cubicle. Girls frowned and glared at Alice as she passed.

'You are going to have to bring the cookies to the Dame,' Mary-Jane said as she walked into her cubicle.

'I know.' Alice was already sweating at the thought.

'Cos if you don't own up, you can be quite sure that a Certain Miss Someone will rat on you. If not to the Dame directly, then to Miss Ash. And it's best the Dame gets it from you directly.'

'I know,' Alice repeated miserably.

Mary-Jane was rooting in her laundry basket.

'Great place to hide something,' she explained, 'no one

will ever look amongst your dirty knickers.'

Alice scrunched up her nose at the thought. Mary-Jane rifled some more and then paused.

'They're not here.' She looked blankly at Alice.

'Very funny, Mary-Jane.'

'No, seriously, they are not here. I put them in this morning after you left, and now they are not here.'

'You didn't take them?' asked the confused Mary-Jane.

'What? No, of course not. I went straight to breakfast.' Alice grabbed Mary-Jane's laundry bag. 'Are you sure they're not in there?' She turned its contents onto the bed. Alice held back while Mary-Jane rifled through the pile of dirty clothes, finding nothing.

'Now what?'

Mary-Jane turned all official. 'I'll have to talk to the Knight Raiders about this.'

'Oh crap, this is all I need. It is bad enough having Martin down on me, but not them as well.' Alice moaned.

CHAPTER 29

Sisterhood

'Right, well this calls for only one thing.' Carrie paced back and forth in the lower dorm. Elton John's *I'm Still Standing* was playing in the background. Alice stood encircled by the Sixth Years with Mary-Jane, Ting and Felicity looking on.

'Alice, you did your part, you are not to blame.' Carrie paused. 'Well you are, but to an acceptable level. Someone is playing with us, and you can be damn sure we will find out.'

Megan nodded supportively.

Alice was grateful for the support. It had been many months since she had stood in the same room with the two seniors. Now here she was again, but there was a completely different air about the place.

'Ting, call in the prefects. We are going to have to do a full dorm search.' Ting nodded and was gone.

'Now, we have half an hour before the study bell to find those cookies, if they are not already eaten or disposed of.'

Megan nodded, crossing her arms.

'Alice, there is no getting away from having to own up to Dame Mary. Sorry, but it is a card we are going to have to play. Dame Mary is a pet, and although you will get the whole disappointment lecture, you will hopefully get off fairly lightly. You might have to take some flack from Martin, but I think you'll live.' Carrie changed out of her slippers and started to lace up her big Timberland boots.

'After all, you are new and it is your first time to get in serious trouble. Ref raiding has been going on for years. Dame Mary isn't a fool. She has known it has gone on, but chooses to ignore it unless someone is caught. But she will have to be seen to take action now that another nun is directly involved.'

'Will Alice be expelled?' Megan asked.

Alice tasted bile in the back of her throat.

'Perhaps, but unlikely, if Alice owns up on her own. No one has been caught for some time. I certainly have no recollection of anyone being caught in my six years. There were some close calls, but never this close. I am not happy it has come to this.'

Alice couldn't speak for fear of bursting into tears.

'Mary-Jane shouldn't have taken you on, Alice. I am not happy that a First Year got to go down unescorted, but that can't be undone now.' Carrie stared at Mary-Jane who was shifting guiltily from one foot to another.

'It was bad luck that Martin had to be involved, and I would strongly suggest you avoid her at all costs in the near future.'

'Since when did Martin start baking anyway?' Megan sniggered.

Carrie was the only one who laughed. 'Ah now, give her her due, she doesn't normally set foot in the kitchen,' Carrie explained. 'The community was probably as surprised as we were to discover that Martin had taken up a spatula.' Carrie tightened her laces with a yank, wrapping them around her ankle twice before tying them home at the back. 'Any thoughts on who might be behind stealing the cookies from Mary-Jane?' Carrie stood up and asked Alice.

Alice shook her head and then remembered something. 'Alexandra,' Alice whispered.

'What about her?' Carrie asked.

'She saw me come out from Mary-Jane's cubicle with some of the cookies, she knew I was going down to raid the Ref last night. Well, I suppose everybody did, but nobody knew I had succeeded. Not till now. Alexandra saw me leave Mary-Jane's cubicle eating a souvenir cookie, just before breakfast.' Alice paused again before adding quietly, 'She's had it in for me from the start.'

'Well, we can't be seen to hone in on just Alexandra, or we will have Miss Ash to contend with.' Carrie looked at Alice. 'You did know that Alexandra is related to Miss Ash?'

Alice stared back dumbly.

'Ah, I see . . . well, you know now. Not sure of the specifics, not that it matters. We have to make it look like a genuine dorm search.' Carrie finished tying her laces and pulled her socks up tight. 'Although, if I'm honest, I would have to agree with you. That Certain Miss Someone has been trouble for you from the word go.'

Ting stuck her head in the door. 'The prefects are ready in the big dorm.'

'Right, let's go.' Carrie clapped her hands together. 'Best to get back to your cubicle, Alice, and do as you are told. No interruptions now, just follow any orders. We need to get moving on this quickly.'

Alice followed behind the group of seniors marching up the stairs behind Carrie and into the Big Dorm. Alice thought it ironic that Queen's *Another One Bites the Dust* was playing in the background. There were some strange looks from the other students as the group made their way into the centre of the dorm and stopped as if to attention.

'Okay everybody, listen up,' Carrie bellowed. The music stopped. 'This is a full cubicle inspection. Everybody is to return and stay in their own cubicle and not to move. All curtains are to be left open so we know you are not hiding anything. You all know what is going down, so just stay put.'

There was a frantic scattering of girls rushing back to their cubicles. Carrie gave the nod and Megan stood at the main door to prevent anyone escaping and keep watch for Ash. Like a plague of locusts, Carrie and the rest of the prefects worked their way down the dorm, briefly inspecting the cubicles that led to their ultimate goal – Alexandra's cubicle. Alice had already returned to her cubicle and was pulling open her curtain when Ruth appeared, startling her. 'Gosh, Ruth, can you believe what's happening?' she whispered.

'I knew something was going on.' Ruth glanced out the cubicle.

'What do you mean?'

'I got that strange feeling again, as if there is trouble about. Well, if I was to be more specific, your trouble. Weird, huh?'

'Hey let's just add it to the list of "weird" for us both, eh?' Alice joked nervously, glancing out at the search.

'After all, I have been here for years and watched many a girl get herself or others into trouble. But I only know that because I am there when it happens or I overhear other girls talking about it. But with you it's different. I get this sense of foreboding, like my stomach goes all funny and I feel a kind of dread, but don't know what about.'

Alice was touched. 'That's kind of nice, Ruth, but I'm not sure how it is going to help me now.'

'Yeah, I thought so, too, but I was on my way here this morning to talk to you about it when I saw something I thought you should know about.'

Ruth was just about to go on when Alice shushed her. 'Look, there is a bit of a commotion over at Alexandra's cubicle.'

Alice watched as Alexandra had a screaming fit. 'I don't believe it! No! I've been framed. Carrie, I swear, I didn't take them, I don't know how they got there!' Alexandra was pleading with Carrie, who stood with the tub of cookies in one hand, the lid in the other.

'Ha,' Alice said triumphantly. 'I was right.'

'Actually, Alice, you're not.'

Alice turned to face Ruth.

'That's what I have been trying to tell you this morning when I came to see you and you were already gone to breakfast. I saw who took the cookies, and it wasn't Alexandra.'

CHAPTER 30

Cookie Monster

'What do you mean it wasn't Alexandra?' Alice asked forcefully.

Ruth didn't know where to start. Alice looked at her and back at Alexandra, still protesting her innocence. 'Crikey, Ruth, you better spit it out.'

'Alice, I don't know how to say this to you, but it was Gale.'

Alice stared blankly at Ruth.

'When I came to see you, Gale hadn't gone down to breakfast.'

'Yeah, I know, Bess said she had to go to the toilet.'

'She never went.' Ruth glanced over to a now sobbing Alexandra. Carrie, Megan and the other prefects had her surrounded and were belittling her in front of a gathering crowd. Ruth's expression was pained. 'Gale crept into Mary-Jane's cubicle, took the biscuits and planted them in Alexandra's cubicle.'

Carrie and Megan were now dragging the pleading Alexandra down the corridor towards them.

'But why? Why would Gale do that?' Alice snapped. 'No, she wouldn't. What does she get out of it? I mean I sort of get why she might plant them on Alexandra, but why take them in the first place? That would only get me in trouble too.'

Alice glanced back down the corridor towards Bessie's and Gale's cubicles. Bessie had a look of horror as she watched the seniors drag Alexandra, but Gale had a resigned look.

'Oh my God, Ruth. Gale would never be so nasty.' Alice choked. 'Would she?' Ruth shrugged her shoulders.

For a moment Alice thought of running out after Carrie but then there was a part of her that wanted Alexandra to get in trouble. Get what was coming to her. Alice stared down at the tub of cookies Carrie had shoved into her hands as the mob passed her.

'Alice, aren't you going to say something?' Ruth asked. Alice looked at Ruth and, ignoring her, slumped onto her bed, staring down at the cookies.

'Alice, what about Alexandra?' Ruth demanded.

Alice paused a moment, thinking, then spitefully stated 'What about her?'

'No Alice, that's not right. Alexandra has been set up. No matter what you think about her, it wasn't her doing.' Ruth looked on incredulous.

Alice stared ahead unblinking. 'Whatever, Ruth. Alexandra has got what was coming to her.'

'Alice, you don't mean that. You have to confront Gale.' Ruth paced in her frustration. 'You have to confront Gale and clear Alexandra's name. It is the right thing to do.'

Suddenly there was a mad dash of feet. Someone was shouting that Miss Ash was coming, and cubicle curtains were yanked closed. A guilty hush descended on the Big Dorm.

'Why should I believe you, Ruth?' Alice asked in a forced angry whisper. 'Gale is my friend. Bessie and Gale have been there from the beginning. If Gale planted the cookies to spite Alexandra, I am sure she would have told me.'

Ruth stared at Alice. Alice was trembling with rage.

And then Alice's eyes widened. She glared at Ruth. 'It was *you* wasn't it?' That's it. *You* took them, *you* planted them on Alexandra, blaming Gale. You did it because, because . . .' Alice paused, thinking. And then she reasoned. 'Because you're *jealous!*'

'What?' Ruth blinked.

'Yes, that's it. You're jealous. I have been friends with Bessie and Gale since the beginning, sharing everything with them, spending all my time with them. You want me to yourself. You don't want me hanging out with anyone or having any friends.' Alice struggled to keep her voice quiet. 'Everything I am, everything I have, everything you couldn't be. You want it.'

'Alice, no, don't be silly,' Ruth sniffed. 'It's not true. I saw Gale. I swear I did.'

'Liar.' Alice's face was ugly with contempt. 'I don't believe you.'

Ruth's tears began to flow. She sniffed, wiping her nose on the back of her hand. Alice tugged the curtain open again and stepped out into the corridor.

'Alice, please, don't go,' Ruth begged. But Alice was already gone.

★★★

There was no doubt that Alice regretted what had just happened, but it didn't make sense to her that Gale would do something to get Alice in trouble.

Alice felt drained, but there was no more to do now than go and bring the cookies to Dame Mary, avoiding both Sister Martin and Miss Ash at all costs.

★★★

There were no sounds from the corridors. In fact, a surreal quiet had descended on the school. Miss Ash had called study time and the dorms had emptied in minutes. Alice was relieved that she didn't have to deal with any students, all of them enclosed behind classroom doors or gone to the study

hall. Walking the corridor with the tub of cookies, Alice prepared herself for the worst with Dame Mary. Her office stood
between the tuck shop and the door to the Ref. Her door was
always open when she was within, in order to be approach-
able to the students. Right now, Alice would have preferred
to have seen a shut door, but there it was, the door slightly
ajar summoning her. Alice paused. Taking a deep breath, she
stepped up and knocked.

'Come in.'

'It's Alice, Dame Mary.' Alice stepped into the small office.
She didn't know where to look.

'Ah Alice, my dear, what can I do for you?' Dame Mary
smiled at Alice. Alice realised that the Dame had no idea why
she was here. This made her feel even worse. She swallowed
before saying, 'I'm here with Sister Martin's cookies.'

'Oh dear.' Dame Mary pulled up a chair and sat. 'I see,' she
said quietly. Alice hated the disappointment in her voice. The
nun sat and gave a big sigh. 'I have to say I am surprised, Alice.
I thought I had an idea of who might have been behind this.
Sometimes trouble just follows a girl, and I would hope that
it would not follow you.'

Alice lowered the tub and looked at her feet. She could
feel blood creep into her cheeks.

'Alice, dear, look at me when I am talking to you.'

Alice looked up, mortified. Dame Mary was sitting up
straight on the edge of her chair with her hands folded gently in her lap. She looked softly at Alice with a sad mouth.
She paused for effect before adding, 'I must say I am *very* disappointed.'

Alice felt her heart crawl into her throat and swell to almost bursting. She couldn't speak for the dam of tears that
was building behind her wretchedness.

'Alice, we are a small community of nuns, the Enclosure

is our private space, not open to the public or students. It is a blessed and holy place. You could say it is our sanctuary. It is not just about breaking into the food store. For a student to enter the Enclosure, it is a breach of our privacy, a breach of our sanctuary, a betrayal of sorts. Do you understand?'

Alice nodded. A big tear streaked down her cheek. Alice didn't move for fear her dam would burst and, once started, she would be unable to stop.

'Of course, you have done well by stepping forward and taking responsibility for your actions. That can take a lot of courage, especially when I suspect that there were others in-volved – if not directly, then by association.'

She looked unblinking at Alice and nodded, as if in con-clusion, then added, 'Unfortunately for both of us, Sister Martin is going to want to see you and say some more on the matter for herself. You must apologise to her, Alice. Sister Martin is not a baker. When she does, it is something the whole community acknowledges.' Dame Mary smiled. 'But I think one confession is enough for tonight. Sister Martin can wait for now.' She held out her hand. Alice handed over the tub.

Dame Mary looked into the now half-empty tub. She took out a cookie, inspecting it before taking a bite. She gri-maced.

'The sad thing is, Alice, and this can be our own little se-cret, you might well have been doing the community a great service.' Dame Mary chewed with difficulty and swallowed.

Alice moved only when the Dame stood and guided her towards the door. 'Now off with you, Alice. You will be late for study. I will have someone get you when Sister Martin is ready for you. I don't want you to feel you are in a permanent state of disgrace, Alice. After all, it is important that you know you are forgiven. But for that you will no doubt have to receive some form of punishment as deemed fitting by Sister Martin. That will, at least, draw a line under the whole affair and we can all sleep a little bit better.' She patted Alice gently on the cheek.

'Yes, Dame Mary, thank you.' Alice went to step out the door when the Dame added, 'I don't think I need to report this to your parents this time, Alice?'

Alice felt some weight drop off her shoulders. No parents, meant no expulsion or suspension. 'Thank you, Dame Mary.'

'I *will* notify them if anything was to happen again. But I would like to think that there will not be a repeat of this? Do you understand me, Alice?'

'No, I mean yes, of course, Dame Mary,' Alice nodded enthusiastically.

CHAPTER 31

Life without Ruth

Things changed in the days following the Ref incident. Sister Martin had prolonged Alice's agony by waiting a full two days before summoning her. She then had only given Alice detention, dismissing her with a warning, saying something along the lines that waiting had probably been punishment enough for her to think about her actions. Remembering Ruth's feelings towards the nun, Alice had offered to help Sister Martin on the farm or perhaps tend to some of the smaller animals outside of school hours. This had made Sister Martin smile warmly, and Alice found a spark of new respect for the nun. Serving detention was easy, given the alternative.

As for Alexandra, well she became more withdrawn. Girls that she had previously intimidated stood more squarely up to her and didn't tolerate any of her bullying. She was defeated and consequently had become the one to be badgered and baited, mocked and slagged. As time wore on Alexandra spent more and more time on her own. The other girls gossiped about her, but then the novelty wore off. The hockey teams were winning their league and Dame Mary was considering sending a bus of supporters to the next round. This would mean a full day's excursion out to the city of Galway, and many an evening was spent with girls planning what they might wear or how they would spend their allowances.

Miss Ash was seen watching Alexandra and having the occasional private chat, but Alexandra was keeping everybody else at a distance. Alice had been nervous at first, expecting the wrath of Miss Ash, that Alexandra must have sought some support from her, but time passed and there was nothing. Nothing obvious at least. Alice would catch Miss Ash looking at her, but the supervisor never took any action or made any comment. Alice found it quite unsettling.

Gale and Bessie were much the same as ever, though Alice couldn't help but feel that something was different. She couldn't put her finger on it, but she found herself watching Gale closely. Bessie had talked incessantly about the raid and the revenge on Alexandra, but Gale and Alice avoided the subject, talking instead about the new season of athletics, gymnastics, homework, or plans for the Easter holidays.

Alice felt the biggest change was not having Ruth around. She hadn't appeared since their argument, and Alice missed her. Dreadfully. Anxious to see her and talk to her, Alice had tried every means of communicating with her to entice her to come, but to no avail. She had even tried to get herself in trouble with Miss Ash by being cheeky or late for study to see if Ruth's theory was true, that she would appear whenever Alice got in trouble, but it never worked. Either Ruth could sense Alice was not in trouble enough or maybe she knew that Alice was only doing it to call her attention. Either way, Ruth never showed.

The Easter holidays were fast approaching and Alice wasn't sure if she was looking forward to going home. Ruth's lack of contact was beginning to worry her, and she feared that Ruth had found a way to pass on or something awful like that. She hoped she would at least come and say goodbye before she left.

It was a Sunday evening and the girls, having returned from Compline to the dorm, were relaxing before lights out. Compline was evening prayer, and while it was thought a bore to attend, the girls expected it as part of boarding school life in a Benedictine Abbey. It marked the end of the week for the girls and a reminder that they had a new school week ahead of them.

Alice was alone in her cubicle writing a letter home when her fountain pen began to run out of ink. She had been writing to Pete, telling him about the usual school stuff, and how she was looking forward to getting home to see him. Alice wandered down to the kettle room to find someone who might have a spare cartridge. Bessie was stirring her Cuppa Soup, chatting to a few of the other girls who were waiting on the kettle to reboil.

'Hey guys, I've just run out of ink. Do any of you have a spare cartridge or fountain pen I can borrow?'

The other girls shook their heads. Bessie nodded, but added, 'It's not here though, mine is in the study hall, but help yourself if you want to go and get it.'

Alice sighed at the thought of having to go all the way downstairs.

'Why don't you use a regular pen?' one of the other girls asked.

'Nah, I have most of the letter written already and don't want to spoil it now.'

'You could try Gale.' Bessie suggested. 'She might have something in her stationery stash. If you're feeling brave enough to ask.' Bessie smiled as she slurped her soup from her teaspoon.

Wandering her way around to Gale's cubicle, Alice found it empty with the curtain closed. Alice stepped in and scanned the small confines of Gale's private world and her store of collectable stationery on her counter top. Gale was never one for hosting gatherings in her cubicle. It felt strangely uncomfortable to Alice to be there alone.

There was pretty much a bit of everything laid out: pencils, erasers, miniature colouring pencils, fancy toppers, and a variety of stationery with the popular names of Hello Kitty, Snoopy, Care Bears and My Little Unicorn. Alice picked up a tiny pencil case with Love Bear on the front and unzipped it. She found a collection of tiny colouring pencils and heart-shaped erasers inside. Alice smiled at this soft side of Gale and then dropped a miniature pencil which disappeared under Gale's bed.

'Bother!' Alice almost said out loud and got down on her hand and knees to pull up the valance on Gale's bed.

Alice couldn't see the pencil so she stretched a bit further under the bed. Her arm brushed something soft and bulky. Bending lower, Alice took a closer look. There, suspended from the underside of the bed was a small hammock-like net. Alice felt guilty as if she had stepped over an unseen boundary, but her curiosity led her to poke around a bit more. Finding a release cord, Alice opened the net and peered in.

There was a jumble of all sorts. Hair bobbles, patterned socks, a polka-dot hair brush, hair scrunchies, neck scarf and plastic bags with penny sweets, cheese triangles and other tuck. Alice noticed a pair of black fingerless gloves that she recognised as Bessie's and there, much to her surprise, was her missing postcard and nail file. Then she saw a plastic bag that contained a single small but significant item. And despite its now mouldy state, Alice recognised it immediately.

'What are you doing?' Gale was standing above Alice, glaring down at her. Alice jumped up mortified.

'Sorry, Gale, I was looking for an ink cartridge. You weren't here and I . . . I dropped a pencil.' Alice held out the tiny Love Bear colouring pencil that she had found under the hammock.

'You have *no* right to be in here.' Gale's cheeks burned crimson.

Alice knew this was true, but something that was bothering her outweighed any trespassing issues that Gale might have. 'Gale, what are you doing with Bessie's gloves and my post card? Isn't this one of Martin's cookie?' Alice held out the cookie.

Gale's eyes darted to her bed. Her face blanched.

'Ruth was right all along! You did take the cookies from Mary-Jane and plant them on Alexandra,' Alice concluded forcefully.

'What . . . no, that's not Martin's. I . . . I made them in Home-Ec,' Gale stammered, and then asked 'Who's Ruth?'

Now it was Alice's turn to be stumped. 'Ruth? Oh that doesn't matter.' Alice dismissed Gale's question. 'We haven't baked cookies yet in Home-Ec. The last time we baked anything there we made scones, and you burnt yours,' Alice hissed.

'You're lying. You took the cookies. My God, Gale, why? After all this time you let me think it was Alexandra, let *us all* think it was Alexandra.' Alice was shouting now, she felt sick. How Ruth had told the truth, how they all had been so cruel to Alexandra. How Gale had betrayed them all, betrayed her and Bessie.

Gale grabbed the pencil from Alice, shoving her. 'Get out of my cubicle.' Alice stumbled backwards.

'Gale, you have to own up. Tell Carrie and the Knight Raiders. If you don't, I will.'

'Ah sod off, you and Miss Goody-Two-Shoes.' Gale grabbed the cookie from Alice. 'It's just your word against mine. You can't prove this is Martin's cookie. Anyway I was doing you a favour, landing Alexandra in it. Silly cow that she is. She deserved everything that was coming to her. And Mary-Jane thought she was so smart hiding them in her laundry bag. Stupid git.'

168

Alice couldn't believe what she was hearing. 'Does Bessie know?'

'What, Bessie? That girl wouldn't ·notice if someone ripped her arm off and hit her with the wet end. Dumb as two planks with a lump of too nice in the middle, that one.'

Gale's face had turned red as she rolled out her thoughts on Bessie. She was just about to go on when the curtain of the cubicle was slowly pulled back to reveal a small crowd that included a pale-faced Bessie and a steaming Mary-Jane. From the look on their faces they had heard everything Gale had said. Bessie was too shocked to say anything. Mary-Jane, on the other hand, couldn't wait to let rip. And let rip she did.

CHAPTER 32

Language Room Shuffle

The quietness of the corridors followed Alice as she stole nimbly down the stairs towards the TV room to try and find Alexandra. Mary-Jane had taken Gale to the lower dorm to face Carrie, and Alice had had an overwhelming urge to seek out Alexandra. She wasn't sure what she was going to say to her when she found her, but she decided that she would figure that out when she did.

On asking around for her, a Second Year said she thought she was down in the piano room. Alice had quickly made her way down the stairs, but opening the door a crack, she was met with pitch black and quiet. Alice paused; she felt sick, a mixture of guilt and regret stewing away within. She had to find Alexandra. Apologise somehow. Pausing, trying to think where she might be, Alice heard the loud sound of a chair falling somewhere in a room ahead. She could hear muffled voices and low, strained whispers. Tiptoeing, Alice moved up close to the language room door. She could see a faint light under the crack in the door, shadows moving from within. Opening it quietly, Alice peered in to find Alexandra being wrestled by Paddy-John. Alexandra whimpered and pushed him away. Paddy-John stumbled against the teacher's podium. He balanced himself and, as if to regain composure, brushed his hand through his tussled hair. A cold night breeze blew the curtains into a dance around an open window. Paddy-John lunged again towards Alexandra. She squealed in fear.

Alice looked on as Paddy-John tripped over himself and had to concentrate to compose himself. Alice thought to herself: *He's drunk. Crazy fool.*

Paddy John grabbed Alexandra's wrist.

'Leave her alone, Paddy,' Alice called out .

Paddy-John stopped and glanced over at Alice.

'Hey there, little one, want to have some fun?'

Alice stepped back, hesitating. Alexandra resisted his grip, squirming, her eyes pleading with Alice to do something.

'What's going on here?' The deep, authoritative voice of Sister Martin loomed suddenly from behind. Alice turned to find the fuming nun standing at the door.

Alexandra and Paddy-John stopped. Taking advantage of the distraction, Alexandra pushed him away and stepped in closer to Alice. Without a word, Alice reached for Alexandra's hand, gripping and squeezing it reassuringly.

'Ah Sister,' Paddy-John slurred. 'Come in, come in. Alex here and I were going to have a bit of a party.' Paddy-John gestured at the air for her to come in as he negotiated his balance.

'Paddy-John Murphy, you have some nerve sneaking in here in the middle of the night.'

Sister Martin stood tall and calm in front of him with her hands hidden beneath her habit. 'Girls, outside, I will deal with you in a minute.' Sister Martin nodded to Alice and Alexandra.

'Shuur, Sister, we were just about to have a bit of fun.' Paddy-John swung his hips mockingly at Sister Martin.

Sister Martin stared at him. 'This is no laughing matter Paddy-John. You need to get yourself home. I don't want to see you around here again. Ever. Your father will be hearing from me.'

Alice and Alexandra had not moved. Sister Martin nodded towards the door.

'Go on now, girls, you have seen enough.'

'How's about a bit for yourself, Sistah?' Paddy-Joe was

laughing as he pulled clumsily at the belt of his trousers.

Sister Martin took a step towards Paddy-John, placing herself between him and the girls. Slowly from within her habit she revealed the long steel barrel of her shotgun.

The girls gasped.

'Put it away, Paddy-John, or I'll put it away for you.' She cocked the barrel at him adding, 'Permanently'.

Alice felt a warm wave of glee seep upwards from her stomach, bursting out of her into a wide impressed smile. Alexandra was slack jawed. Paddy-John stumbled out the open window.

The girls stood paralyzed, dumbly transfixed, gaping at Sister Martin.

'Lucky for you girls it's still lambing season,' Sister Martin said casually. She hid the weapon again 'We lost a few lambs to a fox, had hoped to get him this evening, didn't expect to be using it on a wild dog though.' She nodded towards the direction in which Paddy-John had fled. 'Now off with you, it must be past bedtime,' she added as she herded them out of the language room. 'I'll close up here.'

The girls hurried out into the corridor, happy to escape. The two slowed down as they made their way back round the corner towards the music room. Both realised it was just the two of them now, and each was willing the other to say something.

'Alexandra, I don't know where to start.' Alice smiled sheepishly.

'Perhaps I can help you there, Miss Stone.' Miss Ash stepped quietly out from the music room.

'Alexandra, get upstairs, I'll deal with you later. Miss Stone and I are going to have a little chat.' Alexandra hesitated and was about to say something when Miss Ash glared at her 'You know I don't like having to repeat myself, Alexandra, now get!' Miss Ash shoved Alice roughly towards the Music Room door.

'Please, Miss Ash,' Alice pleaded. 'You've got it all wrong. *We all* got it wrong.' Alice resisted the pull of Miss Ash and spoke to Alexandra. 'Alexandra, I know it wasn't you who took the cookies. Everybody knows.' Miss Ash was shoving Alice with more force now. 'It was Gale all along, Alex, I'm so sorry.'

'You will be by the time I'm finished with you.' Miss Ash had Alice now by the scruff of the neck tugging her. 'You're a no-good-waste-of-space, Alice Stone. You are not wanted here and obviously not wanted at home either. You must know your parents would only send you to boarding school because they do not love you. Sure, they weren't even bothered enough to bring you here themselves '

Alexandra found her voice. 'Please, Miss Ash, stop.'

Her beseeching was drowned out by a bellow from Sister Martin as she stormed in on the fracas.

'*MISS* Ash, that is ENOUGH.'

Miss Ash froze and slowly released her hold on Alice, who quickly side-stepped towards Alexandra. 'Sister Martin, I just caught Alice bullying Alexandra and was about to re-move her,' Miss Ash mumbled. Alice eyes pleaded with Sister Martin. The startled Alexandra moved in closer to Alice and unexpectedly slipped her hand into Alice's, returning a reas-suring squeeze.

Sister Marin ignored Miss Ash. 'Off upstairs with you both, now. I think you have had more than enough for one evening.' She then turned back to Miss Ash.

'Miss Ash, I am sure Dame Mary will be very interested to hear your version of events this evening, I know I am.' She guided the shamefaced Miss Ash in the opposite direction.

★★★

It was decided between Sister Martin and Dame Mary that some grievous lecturing, followed by some extra in-house cleaning chores for Alexandra and Alice would be punishment and example enough. Dame Mary, ever wise and calm, thought it was a good thing that the girls work it out together. She explained that they did not want other students thinking it was acceptable to be downstairs after lights out and be seen to encourage visiting local boys. There had to be some come-uppance. Alice offered to do Alexandra's chores in an effort to make amends, and this gesture in turn helped ease any remaining resentment that Alexandra had towards her.

Miss Ash was not let off so lightly. It was not the first time that she had threatened a student, but it was the first time someone in authority had witnessed her methods. It was all dealt with quietly enough, and when the girls returned after the Easter holidays Miss Ash was on her best behaviour. Rumours ran riot as to what might have been said to her. As for Paddy-John, he wasn't seen working on the estate again.

It was revealed that Miss Ash was actually an aunt of Alexandra's, being the only sibling and sister of Alexandra's father. Both of Alexandra's parents had been killed in a car accident, after which Alexandra became the ward of Miss Ash, who did the bare minimum to meet her obligations as a guardian to Alexandra, and there was no love lost between them. Alexandra in fact had a deep dislike for Miss Ash, but with her aunt using the inheritance as a hold on her, she had to wait until she came of age to be free of her cruel relative.

'Crikey,' Bessie said in sympathy with Alexandra. 'I can't imagine what it must be like to lose both your parents and then have a battleaxe like Ash to look after you. Sounds like a Brother's Grimm fairytale.'

'She would be all nice as pie to the adults,' Alexandra explained. 'And she was very clever to hide any nastiness she had. I couldn't believe it when she took a job as supervisor here. Of course, Dame Mary is aware of her relationship with me, but it was thought it would be in everyone's interest not to know about it.' Alexandra paused, then smirked. 'Oh, Bessie, you should have seen the look on her face when Martin burst in.'

'Oh to have been a fly on the wall of Dame Mary's office for that meeting,' Bessie offered, linking her by the arm.

CHAPTER 33

Kleptomaniac

It seemed a natural course for Alexandra to become a new friend to Alice and Bessie. The relationship between them and Gale was more strained. At first Gale had denied everything, but Mary-Jane's interrogation soon had Gale in tears, and it all came out in an open confession.

From the beginning of first term Gale had been helping herself to odds and ends from other girls' cubicles – things that weren't necessarily valuable but were attractive to Gale for only reasons she would know. Carrie didn't go into it much, but when Mary-Jane called her to Gale's cubicle and the hammock under Gale's bed was revealed, Carrie guessed what was going on.

Gale had returned what she could, and was making up for it by taking on other girls' chores of table-clearing, dorm-sweeping and anything Carrie deemed fit.

Stealing was nothing new to boarding school but there were levels of tolerance, and consequences for any one getting caught.

Alice, Bessie and Alexandra were out taking a walk before study time. Alice was trying to explain to Bessie what conclusion Carrie had come up with. 'A maniac?' Bessie was shocked to hear the latest diagnosis on Gale.

'No, Bessie, a KLEPTO-maniac.'

'What in God's name is that?'

'Someone who steals things without really knowing they are doing it.'

'Isn't the common name for that *thief?*' Alexandra asked, still feeling some bitterness.

'Well, not when it comes to being a klepto.'

'Carrie says that stuff gets taken all the time in boarding school, but a klepto is someone who takes stuff and most of the time doesn't even know they take it. It is a condition.'

'A condition? Like, being sick or something?' Bessie was genuinely concerned.

Alexandra grunted.

'No, not sick.' Alice paused. 'Not in the sick like dying or mental sick way. Well, not really. What I mean is that it's like a compulsion. They can't help themselves.'

'Oh, so Gale didn't really mean to take the cookies and all the other stuff?'

'It would certainly seem that way. Either way, Carrie says that the Dame is happy that the students deal with it. Miss Ash can't say boo after her run in with Martin. Looks like Gale might get off easy enough anyway.'

'But if she was keeping the stuff all together, stashed like, in the net under her bed, surely she knew herself it was there and that she was the one who took it?' Bessie asked. 'I mean, how could she *not* know that she had taken the stuff? It was right there under her bed all the time!' Bessie yanked a leaf off a shrub as they passed by and began to tear it into little pieces. A silence fell between the girls as they made their way towards the back stairs.

'I know. I found that hard to understand, too. But I suppose it is a bit like you and that leaf there.' Alice pointed at what was left of the leaf in Bessie's hand. Bessie and Alexandra looked down at the small shreds.

'What do you mean?'

'Well you probably weren't thinking about it when you took the leaf. But now that I have pointed it out to you, you are very aware of it and now you have the dilemma of what to do with it.'

177

Alice paused at the bottom of the steps. Bessie stood staring down at what was left of the leaf.

'What are you going to do with the pieces now?' Alice asked coolly.

Bessie stared at her. 'I am, um? What do you mean? They're just bits of leaves.'

Alexandra looked confused, not knowing where this was going.

'Yeah, but we are going into school and, now that you are aware of them, what are you going to do with them? Throw them on the ground, find a bin for them, put them in your pocket?'

'Ah stop, Alice, you're not making any sense.' Bessie shoved Alice and, laughing, put the shredded leaf into her pocket.

'See, if I hadn't pointed out that I had noticed the leaf you probably would have just discarded the bits, but as I did, you had to make a conscious decision of what to do with them. I suppose that is what happens for Gale.' Alice started up the steps again and Bessie followed.

'Gale was taking stuff unknowingly, but when she realized she had it, I suppose she couldn't very well hand the stuff back or own up to it. So she had to hide it.'

'But surely she must have known about some of the stuff?' Alexandra interrupted. 'You mean to tell me that she took all that stuff, the good stuff and the crap, the postcards, the hair bobbles, the tuck, *even the cookies,* never once knowing what she was doing?'

Bessie raised her eyebrows.

Alice didn't say anything. She wasn't so sure herself.

CHAPTER 34

Sixth Year Party

Preparations for the annual surprise Sixth Year party had begun. Fifth Years, the organisers, had become very secretive, huddling in cubicles conducting secret meetings. Some juniors had spotted one or two of the Fifth Years sneaking into the back kitchen accompanied by Sister Valentine, and that was a real giveaway.

As a celebration of their last year, Sixth Years became the honoured guests to a banqueting feast that was planned, organised and served by the Fifth Years late into the summer term. It always took place on a Friday – that much everyone knew. It was the one day when there was no study period, and it allowed the Fifth Years to arrange a full evening of dining, games and festivities.

Each fifth year class liked to try and outdo the previous, knowing that they, in turn, would be the honoured guests the following year, thus wanting to set an example of what they might expect in turn. Great themes were invented, decorations made, and menus planned. For the Fifth Years it was an educational, and stressful, experience. Home economics students came to the fore, taking over from the sporty girls for once. For the rest of the school the weeks leading up to the event became a tease. As the weeks passed they thought each Friday was the day, only to be disappointed until there were only a few Fridays left and exam time was approaching. Finally the day would arrive with girls lined up waiting to go into the Ref.

Spring term of 1984 was no different. A few Fifth Years were planted at the front of the queue and gave the signal to open the door to the Ref. A great wave of excitement and celebration ripped through the gang of girls, with feet pounding and stomping on the metal stairs. There was great shoving and pushing as the girls hurried in and gave great gasps as they glimpsed the decorations and plates of treats on the tables.

The First Years were bursting with excitement. As it was their first Sixth Year party, they had no idea what to expect and made their way, pushing among the excited group as it scampered into the transformed Ref.

Giant oriental lanterns hung from the ceiling, with images of dragons and Chinese writing. The tables were decorated with bamboo placemats and chopsticks, with red and white confetti scattered on top. Place names written in Chinese and English marked each girl's setting.

'This is amazing.' Bessie was bouncing with excitement. 'It's like something out of China Town. I wonder did Ting help in sourcing the decorations?'

Alice wasn't paying much attention to Bessie as she was distracted with watching for Gale. Spotting her on the stairs, Alice waved her over.

Gale, Bessie and Alice chatted with each other, taking sneaky pre-Grace pickings from the bowls of prawn crackers when a hush spread throughout the big room as Dame Mary walked into the Refectory with a big, knowing grin. All the girls stood to attention and waited for one of the Fifth Years to lead her to the Top Table where the Sixth Years now sat beaming with delight. It was the only time of the year when Dame Mary joined the girls to dine and it was a big thrill for all the girls to have her in the room with them. Having said Grace, Dame Mary opened her hands as a signal to begin. Of course it meant that the festivities were fairly controlled and conducted in a mannerly way, but as soon as the meal was finished and the formal presentation of keepsake gifts given by the Fifth Years to the Sixth Years over, Dame Mary gave Grace after Meals and she left the Ref with a great cheer from all. Thereafter the chaos commenced. Food fights were strongly forbidden, and so any antics were taken outdoors.

Invariably it involved the Sixth Years and the lake.

Bessie and Alice had already decided to tackle Carrie. Gale was sheepish at first, but Alice reassured her that if anyone was forgiving and game, it would be Carrie

'Anyway, it will take all of us to take *her* on,' Alice joked.

Other girls had planned similar attacks on other Sixth Years, so an impromptu mission was coordinated as soon as the feast was finished to chase, capture and manhandle the sixth years into the lake for a dunking. Of course, the First Years couldn't succeed without the help of a few others. The sixth year party being a day of common ground and comradeship, Mary-Jane, Ting and Felicity were in on the game. However, plans do not always follow through, and it wasn't long before Carrie had managed to shake off an unfit Bessie and Gale on the Gothic path. Alice found herself chasing Carrie toward the boathouse, with Mary-Jane, Alexandra and some others bringing up the rear.

Squeals of laughter and jollity filled the air as other girls chased Carrie's classmates back along. Carrie's smoking habit and lumbering gait soon got the better of her, and the distance between her and Alice shortened. Alice caught up with her, running along the side of the lake. Carrie decided to rethink her strategy and stopped dead just at the water's edge.

'I know what you are up to, Just-Billy, but if you take me down, you are coming with me.'

Carrie stood firm and raised her fists, jokingly challenging Alice to take a step towards her. Alice wasn't so confident now. Felicity and Ting were fast approaching with Mary-Jane and Alexandra behind. Carrie weighed up her chances and tried a different tack. 'Alice, you know I like you, but you do this and I might have to change my mind.'

Alice smiled, knowing she was joking. 'Sorry, Carrie, has to be done.' With the arrival of the other girls, and with a charging shout, all the girls jumped Carrie.

Next thing the girls were in a heap in the lake, soaked and laughing their heads off. There was great shouting and merriment when Ana Bamway arrived, her large frame easily tossing and defending as she battled her way through the water. Carrie was well and truly ducked, and now the event turned into a massive water fight. Jumping again onto Carrie's back, Alice dragged her backwards and the two toppled plunging beneath the surface.

There was a sudden cry of pain. Alice came up spluttering to find Carrie hobbling toward the shore complaining loudly.

'Holy crap, my foot!' She slumped down at the shore and was taking a closer look while a circle of dripping wet girls surrounded her. A chorus of 'Ughs' and 'Yeuchs' filled the air.

'Ah gross.' Carrie grimaced as she inspected her bleeding foot. There was an ugly slash seeping blood along her calf. Alice was mortified. 'Oh my god, Carrie, I'm so sorry. Is it bad?'

'Oh, that looks like it will need stitches.' Megan had arrived and was peering in over the circle.

'D'ya think?' Tanya looked up at her.

'I'm only saying . . .' Megan, offered but Carrie interrupted her. 'Sorry girls, the party is over. This girl needs a hand-up and a shoulder to get back. I think Megan is right.' Carrie attempted to stand and winced. Ana moved in beside her and threw Carrie's arm around her shoulder, bearing most of Carrie's weight. There was a swarm of girls in to assist her.

Alice stood back, not knowing what to do or say. She

watched as Carrie and others followed up along the avenue back towards the Abbey.

They were like an army of wet rats as they squelched along, and a cool breeze blew down the valley, chilling them as they slowly and clumsily made their way back into the school. Miss Ash greeted the girls scornfully, complaining of the wet and chaos as girls struggled up the stairs, some making a dash for the showers and others retreating to their cubicles.

Usually attempts would be made to conceal a not so seriously injured party, but as the blood spots left a trail behind a weakening Carrie, it wasn't long before Miss Ash was there, ushering Carrie to the infirmary and instructing Ana to go and ring the bell for Dame Mary. Alice, Gale and Bessie slopped their way up the stairs, eventually dragging their sodden forms to the lower dorm. For once, the dorm was silent. Megan stood guard at the door.

'Carrie has to go into Clifden for stitches. Dr. Bell is out on call so Ben has to take Carrie to the surgery there. It'll be quicker than waiting on an ambulance to come here.'

Alice felt nauseous on hearing the word ambulance. 'Is anyone going with her?'

'No, Ash wouldn't let anyone go. Enough trouble for the day without dragging others out into the night. Carrie said she would be alright, but I think she might have liked the company.' Megan checked over her shoulder. 'Not easy acting tough when you have an open wound, eh?' she whispered.

Bessie's teeth had started to chatter. 'I need a shower before I freeze. There isn't anything we can do now – we'll just have to wait. Come on, Alice, we can check on her again in the morning.'

'You go on. Someone has to go with Carrie.' She ran down the stairs, jumping two at a time, dashed out the back and raced to the pickup point where she spotted Ben and his car, the motor running.

'Ben, wait,' Alice called. She rushed up to the window and, seeing a pale-looking Carrie, almost lost her nerve.

'Well what is it, child?' Alice nearly dropped when she saw Sister Josetta, the infirmary nun, seated next to Carrie.

'Sorry, Sister, it was all my fault, and I was wondering if – I mean, may I go with Carrie?' Alice politely requested, trying hard to control her chattering teeth.

CHAPTER 35
A Stitch in Time

Bessie felt so much better after a hot shower, body scrub, her hair washed and conditioned. It took an age to scrunch blow dry, and now that she was dressed and ready for bed, she was eager to get a cup of hot noodles. Her plan was to simply snuggle up with her hot water bottle in her sleeping bag *and* duvet, and her latest book, *Flowers In the Attic,* after a quick catch up while she had her noodles.

The Sixth Year party had been a great evening, but it was a pity it ended with such a disaster. Gale was not in her cubicle so Bessie made her way toward the kettle room at the end of the dorm where there was yet again a queue for hot water. The group of girls, Gale amongst them, surrounded Tanya as she updated the girls with the latest news from the Sixth Year dorm.

'Seven stitches?' One of the girls scrunched her face at the thought. 'Gosh, for someone so small, Alice's causes a lot of trouble.'

'Is Carrie on crutches?' a Second Year asked. Tanya went into detail of how Carrie's leg was bandaged. 'And she had to get a tetanus injection.' Tanya pointed towards her rear end, exaggerating a jabbing movement for effect.

'When did they get back?' Bessie asked, wanting to find Alice to hear all the gory details.

'They came back a short while ago. Carrie isn't too uncomfortable, but is looking forward to slagging Alice off for having to get a tetanus shot.'

'How did Alice explain herself at the surgery?'

'What do you mean?'

'Alice, you know, when she went into the surgery. Surely they wanted it explained how Carrie got injured?'

'Alice didn't go to the surgery with them.' Tanya wasn't sure what Bessie was getting at. 'It was just Carrie with Sister Josetta. Ben drove them.'

'But Alice left to go with them. After being at the lake.'

'Well, Carrie is just back and didn't say anything about Alice.' Tanya walked out of the kettle room.

Bessie scurried after her. 'Well, I haven't seen her all evening. She hasn't been in the showers and her cubicle has been empty all the time.'

Tanya saw the angst in Bessie's face. 'We better double-check with Carrie. Just to be sure,' she said, frowning.

Tanya and Bessie left the Big Dorm, checking into Alice's cubicle again, and headed down to the Lower Dorm. They both glanced at each other for support before knocking at the door. The upbeat tones of Michael Jackson's *Beat It* could be heard from within.

Megan answered the door. 'No visitors this evening,' Megan announced in a posh voice. 'Carrie will *gladly receive* you tomorrow,' adding quickly with a grin, 'Bring a treat.'

Bessie looked at Tanya, waiting for her to say something. 'Megan, as much as we would love to see Carrie, we are actually looking for Alice.'

'Huh?' Megan grunted dumbly, hands on her hips. 'You hardly think the main perpetrator of the crime is in here hanging with Carrie.'

'Megan, quit fooling around. So she didn't go to the surgery with Carrie and Sister Josetta then?' Tanya looked at an agitated Bessie.

Megan turned in toward the dorm and shouted above the music, 'Carrie, did Alice go with you guys to the surgery tonight?'

Carrie called back from her cubicle, 'No, why?'

Bessie's stomach churned.

'This is not good. Megan, we have to see Carrie, it's urgent.' Tanya shoved in past Megan and Bessie followed sheepishly behind.

Carrie appeared with two crutches as she hobbled towards the ghetto blaster and switched off the whooping Michael Jackson. 'What's up, Tanya?' Carrie looked from one worried face to the other.

'Sorry, Carrie, I know you have enough on your plate this evening, but it's Alice, she seems to be missing.'

Once Bessie had given her account of Alice leaving to try and travel with Carrie, and Carrie had explained that she had, indeed, asked Sister Josetta to come along, but that she had been turned back, the girls realised just how long Alice had been missing.

'Jeez, what time was that?' Tanya asked.

'Must have been sometime after eight,' Carrie guessed.

'More like nine I think,' Bessie offered. 'By the time we all got up from the lake you got into some clothes and Sister Josetta had organised Ben, it was pretty much near lockup.'

'I think you're right, Bessie.' Carrie hobbled up the stairs. 'And my money's on her still being outside. Tanya get the spare key, bring Ana with you, you know what to do.' Tanya nodded and ran up the stairs two at a time into the Big Dorm.

'What about Miss Ash? Shouldn't someone get her?' Bessie was confused as to what Carrie was planning.

'No, Bessie, not for now. I think we will handle this one – Alice has been in enough trouble this year.' Carrie was hobbling back towards her cubicle.

'I don't understand. I mean, what if she is lost or, or, run away?' Bessie was distraught.

'I somehow don't think our Alice is the running-away

sort of girl. If anyone can find her, Tanya can. Having Ana with her is good backup. That girl doesn't say much, but if you ever needed a Knight buddy, Ana is your girl. Don't worry, Bessie, we will find her, and way before we have to bring Ash or Dame Mary in on the picture.'

Bessie fretted, deciding to go and find Gale, preferring to have someone to share her stress with rather than being alone in her own or Alice's cubicle.

★★★

Gale kept busy with filling the kettle, making tea and running errands for prefects. Alexandra and Bessie ate their way anxiously through the wait. They sat in Alice's cubicle, discussing all the possible disasters that might have befallen her, and any consequences that might result, munching their way through what tuck they had left. When Miss Ash started to call lights out they quickly made up her bed to look as if she was already asleep. Both girls returned to their own cubicles, pretending to do the same there and waited a bit before sneaking back up the corridor to Alice's cubicle to wait together.

It seemed an age, but it wasn't long when the curtain was dragged back and a shivering Alice was led into her cubicle by Tanya and Ana.

Alice looked like death. Sodden and muddy, her lips were blue and she could barely stand. Bessie and Gale jumped up to help.

'My God, where was she? What happened?' Bessie whispered. Ana laid Alice on her bed and started to strip off her wet shoes and socks.

'Found her heaped up by a log near the mountain Pokey. More of that later – for now Alice needs a good hot shower and something warm to eat. I think we are going to have to call Sister Josetta this time. I think she got a good bang to the head.' Tanya paused. 'But before I do, no mention of Alice being stuck outside. There will be too many questions of how we got out to find her. We'll just have to put it down to her catching a chill from all the antics this afternoon and the water fight. Banged her head when she slipped. All agreed?' Tanya stared hard at everyone.

'Agreed,' they answered in unison.

★★★

Sister Josetta, like Miss Ash, had complained about the late hour, and grumbled at the inconvenience until she took a look at Alice. Then she quickly turned quiet and attended to her. After she saw the pale, limp form in the bed, and taken Alice's temperature, Dr Bell was called out so that the proper medicine could be administered and care instructions issued. There was a lot of whispering in the dorm that night as a fever took Alice, and Sister Josetta monitored her through the early hours. Bessie and Gale eventually fell into an exhausted sleep after trying to stay awake in their own cubicles fretting over her. Miss Ash gave stern instructions that all girls were to go to bed and there was not to be a sound.

The morning brought a bright new day, and Dame Mary.

Alice slept through her visit and the reassurances of both Dr Bell and Sister Josetta.

It was much to the relief of everyone when she finally woke and, while she had not fully recovered, she was more alert then she had been. Her temperature had dropped and, despite having an impressive head bruise by the second day, she didn't look too much worse for wear. Alice was allowed to stay in her own cubicle instead of being brought to the infirmary, with strict instructions to rest. Bessie, Gale and

Alexandra had popped in. Much to their relief, Sister Josetta allowed them some time to visit while she left to attend to the infirm nuns in the Enclosure.

Alice smiled meekly at Gale. It was the first time that they were all together alone since the fall-out.

'Alice, you gave us a right scare,' Bessie scolded jokingly.

'Yeah, you had the whole school talking about you, again!' Alexandra teased, adding, 'JB.'

'JB?'

'Yeah, that is what Carrie called you this morning,' Bessie explained. 'You know, as in Just Billy.'

Alice answered with a coughing fit, smiling in between spluttering. 'JB, I like that.'

'Sure, JB, *Just Bananas* is more like it,' Bessie teased. 'You are one crazy girl, Alice Stone.'

'How is Carrie?' Alice croaked.

'Oh, she is fine, off the crutches now, finding it easier to hobble holding on to a few slave juniors,' Bessie joked. 'Seriously, though, she was up earlier to check on you. How *are* you feeling?'

'Pretty foolish,' Alice said. The girls didn't say anything. 'I mean, what eejit gets herself locked out?' Alice fidgeted in the bed.

'I must admit, I am a bit confused as to how you were not able to get back in, or even get anyone's attention,' Gale said. Alexandra frowned at her.

'I know.' Alice thought for a moment. She explained that when she came in from the car, the back gate was already locked, and that her pounding on it had gone unheard. The only visible windows were those of the empty Ref, Library or classrooms. She had tried throwing some pebbles at those, but of course no one was studying late after the Sixth Year party. She really didn't want to have to resort to knocking on a window in the nuns' wing, so had attempted to find another way. First by going up the hillside, omitting that she knew Tanya had gone in that way before, and explained that she couldn't find her way in the dark, just kept tumbling and sliding in the mud, eventually slipping hard enough that she banged her head on one of the old cut logs. 'I must have knocked myself out,' Alice admitted.

'Come on, ladies.' Miss Ash had appeared at the end of the bed. 'Alice needs her rest. It is study time for you lot. You can save your nattering for tomorrow.' She forced a smile at Alice. 'You get some rest now, my dear.'

★★★

Alice was still feeling pretty tired and weak and most definitely homesick. A silence settled in the dorm and Alice tried to get comfortable in her bed. She tossed and turned and could still feel a damp chill in her spine, now exaggerated by the cooling hot water bottle that sat limply by her side. Deciding it was time to put pride aside, Alice leaned over the side of her bed and pulled at the bag underneath that contained the old quilt. It would give her the extra warmth she needed and also the comfort of home that she longed for at that moment. Feeling too weary and sluggish to get out of the bed, she gripped the quilt and pulled it from the bag, snagging it as she did. A tug released it, accompanied by a small ripping sound.

Alice gasped and spread the cover over herself, quickly scanning it as she patted it flat. She thought she had imagined the rip when her eye spotted a torn corner of patchwork. Her fingers stroked the tear when her hand rested on something hidden in the quilt. There was a crinkling sound. Poking around a bit more, Alice found something hidden in a patch in the quilt. Slipping her finger in, she found some paper. She was just about to pull it out when a sudden chill swept into the room. Alice looked up to find Ruth standing by her bedside.

CHAPTER 36

Answers

'Ruth!' Alice was delighted.

'Alice, gosh you really are in a bad way. I am so sorry, I sensed something was wrong, but I ignored it. I was very cross with you, you know . . .' Ruth suddenly stopped and stared down at Alice's bed. 'Where did you get that – I mean . . .'

Ruth was pointing silently at the quilt.

'Ruth, are you okay? Even for a dead person you are looking pretty pale.'

'My quilt, that's my quilt. Where did you get it?'

'What, this? No that's mine, I have had it here since after Christmas, just didn't bring it out till now.'

'No, it's mine, at least it certainly looks like mine, I think.' Ruth sat down on the bed and stroked the quilt, her face contorted as she tried to think. 'At least I am nearly sure it is. I had one just the very same. Even had it here in school.' Ruth paused. 'At least I think I did.' Ruth made a closer inspection of the patchwork pattern and scraps of old material that made up the quilt.

Alice was beginning to wonder which of them might have a fever. She had nearly forgotten about the patchwork pocket and started to poke around again.

'But this has been in my family for ages. It was passed down . . .' Alice paused. 'Ruth, what happened to your quilt when you died?' Alice's head already felt cloudy and muggy after the fever, and this new conundrum wasn't helping.

'I'm not sure. After all, technically I was dead, remember? Why do you ask?'

'Well this one was my grandmother's, and it has been passed on since.' Alice was trying to retrieve the paper that was hidden in the pocket.

'Your grandmother?' Ruth's eyes widened. 'What was her name?'

'Terri, I think. Mum sometimes tells us stories of her ancestry when she's feeling nostalgic.' Alice at last got a hold of whatever was hidden in the folds and started to pull it out of the quilt.

'Come on, Alice, try and remember, what was her full name?'

'Terri, Teresa, Teresa Jackson, and her husband was Stephen.'

'What was her maiden name?' Ruth was getting impatient. 'What *is* that?' Ruth pointed at the paper in Alice's hand.

'Fitz-something,' Alice mumbled, and then went quiet as she read what was on the paper.

'Fitz-what? Was it Fitz-Patrick?' Ruth asked excitedly.

Alice was too distracted by the letter to hear Ruth's question.

'Ruth, you're not going to believe this.' With shaking hands, she handed the letter to Ruth. 'I think this is for you.'

Ruth read it slowly; the words were faded and difficult to read. Alice watched as silent tears streamed down Ruth's face.

'I don't understand. I mean, how can this be?' Ruth sniffled.

CHAPTER 37

Letter to Ruth

My Dearest Ruthy,

There is a vacant empty spot in my heart which you had filled with so much love, and try as I might, my interest in this home has died with you. I dread returning to the empty room where you spent your early years with your bursting smiles and giggles. I am haunted by your constant shadow. And so it is with a heavy heart that I have decided to give my notice.

Forgive me for my cowardliness and not standing firm in September when I should have, you leaving for school and not fully recovered from your cold. I ask myself to this day would it have made the difference if you had waited another week or two to start. Instead I stayed quiet, respectful of your parents' wishes, leaving you go on to that dreadful place with its cold damp walls and bad luck. I know there was all the Troubles here in the City, but my gut told me they should have taken that risk.

Oh, Ruth, when the telegram arrived with the news of your illness I knew it was a bad omen and wanted to go to your side, but your mother wouldn't hear of it. I cannot forgive her for that. I cannot forgive myself. Sure, weren't you as good as my own. My dearest Ruth, Mo Stórín óg, Mo Peata. Many's the night since and I wake thinking I hear you calling my name.

Fr. Hurley says you must be a great saint when God let you suffer so much on earth as all the saints had to suffer. And that you were a great patient, never grumbling. But I fret at the thought of you dying alone, no one there to comfort you, take your dying kiss.

Forgive me, Ruth, for failing you, forgive me for being so selfish in my misery. I pray to the Sacred Heart that you are safe and happy now by His side, and you have found peace and rest until we meet again. I write this now before I leave my position. I will leave it in your quilt. John-Joe was a good man to return it to us after you died. God bless him and his people.

It is the closest I can be to you, knowing my letter will lie within that which hugged you at your last.

Forever yours, Teresa

Alice was very confused, but didn't want to rush Ruth, who had slumped onto her bed, holding the letter limply.

Alice waited, quiet, until a coughing fit overtook her and she could barely catch her breath. Ruth looked up, watching helplessly as Alice hacked and spluttered. Sitting up straight, she tried to reach for air. And then it was over. She took a sip of water from beside her bed, red-faced and out of breath.

Something clicked into place for Ruth, and her face brightened.

'Alice, I remember! I know what happened.' Ruth jumped up with excitement. 'I remember, I remember everything!'

'What do you mean?'

'Your coughing, being sick, the quilt, the letter, *Teresa's* letter. It all makes sense now.'

'What?'

'I got really sick. It had started with a bad cold that I hadn't quite recovered from when I started school here in September 1923. I used to help Sister Brigid on the farm with the milking and small animals. By the November I still had a bit of a cough and weak chest. I caught consumption.' Ruth frowned. 'Gosh, Alice, it was awful. The coughing and the spluttering. There was a lot of blood.' Ruth paused, remembering. 'The nuns were dreadfully worried. Frightened even. It was so contagious. It all happened so quickly. I was put into isolation. Dame Scholastica sent a telegram to Mama and Papa, but it was too late. They didn't get here in time.'

196

Ruth sat down on the bed again. 'Oh, Alice, I was all alone, and the sickness was dreadful. All I wanted was for Teresa to come. It was Teresa who made me the quilt, it was her gift to me on coming to school.' Ruth stroked the faded and worn cover. 'Dear Teresa, she was my nursemaid and nanny, then my confidante. She was always there for me. More like a mother to me than my own.'

'But how did my grandmother get it?'

'Oh, you are a nitwit, Alice.' Ruth was totally enjoying her new revelation. 'Your grandmother and my nurse nanny, they are one and the same.'

'Huh.'

'Teresa, Terri!'

'But how could that be?'

'Teresa was only sixteen when I was born. She worked as a nursemaid for us in Dublin. She stayed on with us for years. I was fourteen when I started school. Both of us hated leaving each other, but Mama and Papa thought it best to prepare me for society and get away from all the politics that was going on in Dublin at the time. It was shortly after the Civil War. Dublin wasn't a great place for a young daughter of a mixed marriage at the time. There were ructions between the Protestants and Catholics. The country was in a heap. The Irish were fighting against themselves.' Ruth picked up the letter again. 'Teresa must have left our household. She must have decided to take the quilt with her.' Ruth paused. 'John-Joe must have sent it to her from school.' Ruth smiled remembering him, and then added, 'She had made it especially for me, sewing each square. What was it she used to say?' Ruth thought for a moment.

'*There's a whole lot of love in that quilt,*' Alice quoted. Ruth gaped at Alice.

'That's right, that's what she used to say.'

The two laughed and joyfully hugged, cheek to cheek, delighted for each other.

Suddenly the two girls found themselves spinning, the cubicle becoming a blur as they whirled round and round. They clung to each other, eyes tight, as everything around them appeared to fall away, flashes of bright light and then darkness engulfing them.

With a sudden jolt it was over as soon as it had begun. Still clinging to each other, the two girls opened their eyes.

'What was that?' Alice felt dizzy and nauseous.

Ruth slowly disentangled herself from Alice's arms and looked around her. Alice followed Ruth's gaze. The cubicle was gone. In fact, the entire dormitory had disappeared. Alice was sitting on a bed, but it was not her bed anymore. It was a four-poster bed with fine linen sheets and starched pillowcases. They were in a large beautiful bedroom. Something was familiar, but Alice couldn't put her finger on it.

'Ruth, where are we?' Alice looked at Ruth. She was fresh and peachy looking. 'Ruth, you look different. Almost healthy!'

Ruth looked at her hands. Felt her face. Reached out and pinched Alice.

'Oh! What was that for?'

Ruth broke into hysterics. 'Alice, this is amazing! I feel alive. She pinched herself. I can feel it, I *am* alive!'

Alice smiled joyfully at her friend, then stopped, 'What does that make me then?' Alice panicked.

'Don't worry, you are fine. Didn't you feel my pinch?' Ruth jumped off the bed and hurried over to the window. 'Gosh, it is as I thought. You'll never believe where we are,' she called over to Alice.

Alice struggled out of the bed and made her way over to the window. She gasped when she recognised the view. There was the parapet and the lake beyond, Diamond Mountain in the distance. They hadn't gone anywhere.

Yet everything was different.

'Look at the avenue trees. See how small they are. And the room. It is as it should be. I mean how it was.' Ruth twirled around the room, picking up trinkets and stroking the furnishings.

'Ruth you're not making any sense.' Alice felt exhausted. She couldn't think. She rubbed her eyes.

'Alice, don't you see? We are still here, we are still in school, only it's not school as we know it.'

'Oh my God.' Alice turned on the spot and took in her surroundings. 'It's a bedroom in the old castle.'

Ruth was nodding, enjoying seeing Alice make sense of it for herself.

'Are we in the past?' Alice whispered, shocked at her own question.

Ruth caught Alice by the arms, twirling her round and round, giggling.

'I do believe we are.'

THE END OF BOOK ONE

Chapter One: Stepping

A lice took in the room in which she and Ruth now stood. This was not the dowdy cramped boarding school cubicle that they had both occupied only moments ago. Nor were they in the big dormitory wing where the students of Kylemore Abbey School for Girls slept. Even Ruth, a ghost at Kylemore since her death there nearly one hundred years ago, was stunned by where they both found themselves.

One minute Alice and Ruth were hugging each other, friends again after a falling out; the next, they are whisked and spun, only to just as suddenly find themselves in a strange luxurious bedroom.

It was an elegantly beautiful room with detailed etched wallpaper and decorative borders. The furniture was old world, a writing desk in the corner. The air was cool but fresh, with a slight hint of perfume. There was an orange glow from a fire in the hearth that made the marbled detail on the surround dance and jig in the light. Alice fingered the soft heavy folds of the velveteen curtains and felt the softness of the rug beneath her feet.

They were definitely no longer in the Big Dorm. And, despite her gut telling her that Ruth was right and that somehow they must have time-travelled into the castle's past, Alice couldn't put any sense or reason to it. She was about to say something to Ruth when she heard approaching steps from outside the bedroom. Someone was coming up the corridor. Alice went to step in closer to Ruth, but froze when she heard the door handle turn. The door opened a fraction, and Alice held her breath. They both stared at each other in a panic. Ruth put her finger to her lips, silencing Alice.

A tiny foot appeared at the threshold as the door was pushed open to reveal a petticoat skirt hem. Then a young girl's voice called suddenly from somewhere else down the corridor.

'Geraldine, come on. Papa has the four-in-hand and the phaeton is waiting.'

The foot stopped at the threshold and then the prettily shoed foot was drawn back into the corridor, and the door closed. Alice sighed, then suddenly the door was pushed in again and a young, beautiful woman stepped into the room. She called back down the corridor, 'They'll have to wait, I'll be there in a minute. I just want to get my new gloves.'

Alice held her breath as the young women stepped into the bedroom. Fearing the worst, she clenched her eyes closed, wishing herself invisible. A second passed and Alice could hear gentle footsteps and swishing skirts as the woman crossed the room. Alice opened one eye. Ruth was pointing at her and laughing.

'Oh, you should see your face. It's alright, she can't see us.'

Alice opened both eyes wide and watched as the young woman rummaged through her dresser and, after pulling out a pair of gloves, turned and hurried out the door again. Alice gasped, realising she had been holding her breath.

'Oh my God,' she whispered, still in shock.

'This is *fantastic*.' Ruth twirled on the spot.

'Ruth, what is going on?' There was some panic in Alice's voice.

'I'm sure I don't know. But one thing I do, and that is I feel *alive* again.'

It was very clear to Alice what she was feeling. Panic had lodged itself in the back of her throat. Time stood still for a moment as the two girls stopped and looked at each other.

'Who was that?' Alice managed eventually breaking the silence.

'The girl in the hall called out "Geraldine". She must be Geraldine Henry. She is one of Mitchell and Margaret's daughters. Ruth moved toward the door to look out.

'Ruth, wait,' Alice said. 'Don't.'

Ruth paused.

'Don't leave the room. Don't leave me . . .'

'Oh, come on, Alice. What are you afraid of?'

Alice wasn't sure. But the unknown frightened her. After all it is not everyday a girl finds herself whisked into the past. Afraid to move, to leave the sanctuary of the room, afraid they might lose the link with her own time, Alice asked, 'Ruth, what if we are stuck here now? What if leaving the room means we are stuck back in time?' Alice scanned the room seeking an exit route.

'Don' be silly,' Ruth tut-tutted, then reconsidered. 'But then again, how can I be sure?'

'I don't like this, Ruth, I want to go back.'

Suddenly Ruth stopped. Alice didn't like Ruth's sudden serious expression, her eyes darting about the room quickly, as if searching for something.

Ruth strode over to the dressing table where she picked up something small and silver and shook it. Alice heard a delicate bell sound. It was a baby's rattle.

'Geraldine Henry,' Ruth stated.

'What?' Alice was confused.

'Geraldine Henry,' Ruth repeated as if the name would make sense of her actions as she shook the baby's rattle again as if for emphasis.

'What about her?' Alice asked.

'The phaeton,' Ruth replied.

'Ruth, please, you are not making any sense.'

'Alice, we have to do something.' Ruth was agitated now.

'What about Geraldine, and this *phantom*?' Alice didn't like the sound of a phantom.

'Geraldine was killed driving one when she visited Kylemore one summer.'

'A phantom? How can you drive a phantom?'

'Oh, Alice, sometimes you can be just plain silly. Not a phantom, *a phae-ton*. It's an open carriage with large wheels and springing base. Driven by one horse and is very sporty. Considered a real high-flyer. Geraldine had it brought over from America.'

Alice was still trying to make some sense of what Ruth was saying when Ruth continued, 'The nuns used to tell us the story as a warning to us girls if we were fool-acting while out riding.' Ruth paused trying to remember. 'Her horse got spooked at Derryinver Bridge. They were thrown from the phaeton. The nanny and Elizabeth survived, but Geraldine was thrown into the river.'

Now Alice was beginning to make some sense of Ruth's ranting.

'They found her a couple of hours later. It was a horrible tragedy for the family, and they say the undoing of Mitchell Henry.' Ruth placed the baby's rattle gently back on the dressing table. 'Alice, we have to do something.'

Alice sat down slowly on the edge of the bed. Ruth paced the room, thinking. Alice ran all this new information through her mind, then quietly said, 'Ruth, we can't.'

Ruth stopped pacing. 'What do you mean?'

The logic was simple for Alice.

'Ruth, we can't change the past.'

'Oh don't be silly. Of course we can. If we are here before it happens, and we know what is about to happen, we can do something to prevent it.'

'No, you don't understand. Ruth, I know we *can* if we choose to, but then by doing that we will change the future.'

Ruth raised her eyebrows, encouraging Alice to go on.

'Ok, say we save Geraldine, then what?' Alice was trying to remain calm.

'Well, she lives then doesn't she?' Ruth stated angrily.

'Yes, but then what?'

'I don't know.' Ruth was getting upset. 'She gets to live. Isn't that enough?'

Alice stood up and stepped forward towards Ruth.

'Ruth I know this must be hard to understand, but I have seen enough time travel movies to know that you don't mess with the past 'cos it will just put the future in a flap.'

Ruth gave Alice a puzzled look. 'You know, like warp it,' Alice explained, 'change it somehow. By saving Geraldine we initiate a whole new time map. What happens to the castle then? The nuns? The school? Us?'

Alice stepped towards Ruth. Ruth stepped gingerly back. Alice extended her hand towards Ruth, pleading with her eyes, willing Ruth to clasp it. Ruth stepped away out of reach. Then taking another step away from Alice she turned suddenly, declaring, 'Maybe I'll get to live too.' And Ruth darted for the door.

To be continued . . .

Acknowledgements

I could not have got this far without my 'Righting Sirens', my own true K-buddies, King-Fixer and the Mini-Me's, and my side-line supporters: the Hobbers, the Skull-ites, Summer Covers, the ever so generous Parson, and my own secret group of Little Testers. To you all, a big Little thank-you, and apologies to any of ye who had to clean up after my tears and tantrums.

Then there are those professionals, and colleagues, who have helped in many ways, both great and small, and I would like to name here. To all the wonderful, spiritual, hard-working, fun-loving nuns, OSB, at Kylemore Abbey, and especially Sister Benedict for her tales of days-of-old and Kylemore historical facts; Kathleen Villiers-Tuthill, whose own book, *History of Kylemore Castle and Abbey* provided the tangible to what I thought was the intangible, and provided great fuel for my own imagination; Dr. Pauline Hughes Ward and Dr John Casey (Snr.), Susan Shields and Gerry MacCloskey for their help in any medical research and background; fellow ink-pushers, Con Hurley, Susanne O'Leary, Elizabeth Rose Murray, Laura Cassidy, Gordon Grant, and Terry Brown. – writer envy and forever wanting to catch your seemingly just-within-reach coat tails has kept me going; mentors and workshop leaders/writers (beyond the decade), but especially Katie Gould, Tessa Gibson, Garlo Gebler, Graham Rawle, Suzanne Power, Malcolm MacClancy and Maurice Sweeney; and last, but by no means least, my own family – Vaj Vaj, Bold Boy, Big Sis and the not so little Littles –

'because of you I did it myself'.

About the author

Lydia Little grew up in Kinsale, County Cork, Ireland. Convincing her parents to send her to boarding school, Lydia attended secondary school in Kylemore Abbey School for girls in Connemara, County Galway, from the ages of twelve to eighteen. Having kept diaries throughout, she still enjoys putting pen to paper, only now her journals are full of plots, scribbles, quotes and new characters, all shouting for inclusion in her new books. After a stint of sailing, living in the UK and a short life as a hotelier, Lydia has returned to West Cork with her husband, three children, three dogs and a mad-eyed cat named Bowie. *K-Girls* is her first novel.

Made in the USA
Charleston, SC
06 September 2013